MORE SECRET FILES OF SHERLOCK HOLMES

Five untold tales of the great detective. In the first, Holmes chronicles to Watson a strange event at a freak show years before he met the good doctor. The second sees Watson throwing a birthday party for his friend — but danger lurks among the festivities. The detective and the doctor play golf at St. Andrews, and then are invited to Paris to solve a most perplexing art theft. Finally, Conan Doyle's Professor Challenger meets the duo, who arrive in the hope of preventing an attempt on his life.

GARY LOVISI

◆

MORE SECRET FILES OF SHERLOCK HOLMES

Complete and Unabridged

LINFORD
Leicester

First published in Great Britain

First Linford Edition
published 2017

A catalogue record for this book is available
from the British Library.

ISBN 978–1–4448–3528–1

Published by
F. A. Thorpe (Publishing)
Anstey, Leicestershire

Set by Words & Graphics Ltd.
Anstey, Leicestershire
Printed and bound in Great Britain by
T. J. International Ltd., Padstow, Cornwall

This book is printed on acid-free paper

The Strange Case of The Wrinkled Yeti of the Club Foot and His Abominable Life

We all know that Watson was often a somewhat less than accurate chronicler of the cases of Sherlock Holmes, whether intentionally or not. Being a Holmes fan and collector for some decades, as well as the author of some pastiches that continue the adventures of the great detective, I was amazed when I came upon this manuscript hidden in an old desk I purchased in a dusty old New England antique mart several years ago. When I got the desk home, upon closer examination I discovered secreted behind the top drawer a slim weatherproof packet that held the following manuscript which I have reproduced herein exactly as written. While I cannot attest to the accuracy of this strange missive, I leave it to your good judgment as to the veracity of the words herein.

From the reminiscences of John H. Watson, M.D.

It is with a heavy hand that I take up my pen to write this particular narration of one of the most intriguing and yet embarrassing aspects of all my chronicles of the cases of my friend, the great detective, Sherlock Holmes. I write these words in the year 1894 to put truth to the tale as I have discovered it from Holmes' very own lips.

I have written previously how my dear friend Sherlock Holmes kept records of his early cases in a large tin box which he once shared with me before he put the box in storage. Sadly, that box went missing as the years passed, a tragic loss to the ages. Whether it resides in some secret vault or even the dark dungeon beneath the Diogenes Club, I do not know. However, the great artist Sidney Paget did make a drawing of Holmes and myself looking through this box, and that illustration even appeared in the May, 1893 issue of *The Strand Magazine*. That issue contained my chronicling of the Sherlock Holmes case 'The Musgrave Ritual'. It took place at the beginning of his career as a consulting detective on October 2, 1879. However, at the time when I was told the story of the Musgrave puzzle by Holmes, he also mentioned in passing even earlier cases that he had been involved in since the start of his career in 1877.

Holmes once made mention to me of these early cases, which he said took place between 1877 and the time of 'The Musgrave Ritual'. The case in question here is the one generally known as that of 'Ricoletti of the club foot, and his abominable wife'. Holmes only mentioned that brief description of the case to me verbally, and no more about it. It is a case yet unrecorded by me, and one that certainly has become one of the most intriguing titles of any of my friend's adventures of these many years — but it would become my most embarrassing and unforgivable of all errors. Let me explain.

It was in May, 1893 when *The Strand Magazine* hit the news-stands containing my chronicling of 'The Musgrave Ritual'. I was proud of that story, for not only did it recount one of Holmes' earliest adventures and appear in print after many years, it formed the backdrop of his early career as a consulting detective illuminating his great genius and talents. Little did I realise at the time the turmoil the publication of that story would cause me.

At the time, I had not seen Holmes for some months. I no longer resided with him at our old Baker Street digs, but with my sweet wife in a small terraced house in central London. Over the years I had been doing quite well chronicling the cases and having them published in *The Strand* through the kind devices of Doctor Doyle, who acted as my literary agent. I often did not receive reaction from Holmes on the publication of these stories, which were fictionalised accounts of his cases — most of the time they were of cases we shared together, and so my notes were quite accurate. But 'The

Musgrave Ritual' was quite different; even unique. That is because it was the one case that Holmes narrated to me verbally. It was in the winter of early 1888 when he had shown me the contents of his large tin box; a box full of his earliest cases. It was a veritable treasure trove, but he did not allow me to go through the contents (as I certainly wished to do), nor to read extracts or make notes. Nevertheless, at the time I was just overjoyed to know the material existed.

From inside that box, he suddenly withdrew a smaller wooden box; and this he did show me, for the contents pertained to Reginald Musgrave's strange problem. Of the remainder of the material in the tin box, I noted many bundled sheets and papers — a mysterious goldmine of Holmes' work before I had ever met him! Sadly, I never actually read a word of any of that unknown material. My friend was usually very tight-lipped about his earliest cases. That box is gone now, lost to eternity. That one instance was the only time Holmes spoke to me concerning his long-time friend Reginald

Musgrave. He told me the story speaking quickly in his usual rapid-fire bursts of frantic energy. I listened in rapt attention as I scrambled to quickly jot down what facts and notes I could glean from him as the words burst forth from his lips. It was difficult for me to keep up with Holmes' quick words, but I did my best to get the gist of the story. In the telling, he also mentioned some earlier cases he had worked on in that early period. He did not go into detail on any of these, merely mentioning intriguing titles or a scant phrase that offered a mysterious tidbit hint. I quickly scribbled these names down into my notes as well, just as I heard them at the time from Holmes' own lips. I realised these might make an intriguing addition to the main story I wanted to tell of Holmes' early days — one of these I had written down as the Ricoletti case.

Over the many years of our association, Holmes rarely mentioned my chronicles of his cases. Oh, for sure he pooh-poohed them as being overly melodramatic and catering to the lowest aspects of popular taste. He even told me that I often played loose with the facts — but I stood firm on the notion that some fictionalisation and dramatic licence were necessary for popular publication. 'That is the problem,' he would reply, then drop the discussion. However, until now he had never complained seriously about any of my chronicles of his adventures. In truth, I believe up until then that he was rather flattered by them, and he did mention I had a certain flair with the pen. But that day in May, 1894 it all changed. I had a visit from Sherlock Holmes to my London apartment, and he was not in the best of moods. I thank my lucky stars that my sweet Mary was away for the week to her sister's house in Surrey so she would not be there to witness my abject embarrassment. My partner, Dr. Philip K. Jones, had taken over my practice for the day so that I was free and quite alone when my surprise guest arrived.

The door knocker boomed in anger that morning, and answering it, I was immediately surprised but delighted to see my old friend Sherlock Holmes framed in the doorway. He stood tall and firm, in deerstalker and Inverness cape, just as I always pictured him in my mind, and he looked well, hale and hearty — but severely troubled.

'Hello, Watson,' was all he said.

'Holmes?' I asked, utterly surprised to see him. He was the last visitor I ever expected these days. We had not seen each other in months and our association had grown sparse, though I missed him dearly. 'Holmes!' I shouted and took his hand, shaking it with a release of my pent-up enthusiasm. 'It is so good to see you!'

'May I come in?' he asked rather tersely. I could see something was severely troubling him. 'There is a matter I must speak to you about.'

'Of course, of course,' I stammered, leading him into my small parlour. 'What can I do for you? You know you only need ask.'

Holmes looked at me sharply. Fierce anger flowed from his eyes for a heartbeat, then it quickly died down and was replaced with a wan smile and a sad sigh. It was that same exasperated look he often gave Lestrade whenever the inspector told him of his theory about some crime, showing his thinking process to be thick as a brick. He was not happy. I grew most unsettled.

I quickly took my friend's coat and then led him to a comfortable seat. I asked if he required a drink and he briskly refused. 'It is so good to see you again, Holmes. So good!'

He gave me a stern look. 'Whatever will I do with you?'

'What do you mean?' I was growing fearful now. 'Have I done something to offend you?' I blurted, alarmed. Of course nothing could be further from my wishes, and while I did not say this verbally, Holmes knew all too well that it was true.

'Watson, Watson, Watson,' he said, shaking his head in dismay, 'I have just read your *Strand* story, 'The Musgrave Ritual'.'

'Was something amiss?' I asked sheepishly, for Holmes had always told me my flair for the melodramatic in my writings and fawning enthusiasm for his methods and talents would land me in trouble one day.

'Amiss! That is how you would put it? It is an unmitigated disaster!'

I looked downward, suitably cha-grinned. I had obviously got some small fact or date wrong. Holmes was a stickler for details; often tiny and insignificant items — or so I often thought — which meant so very much to him. And yet, I realised with a bit of trepidation that my notes from this particular case were not as full as others, for they had been scribbled in haste many years before, and only after Holmes had narrated the particulars to me that winter in 1888. Truth be told, I often had trouble reading my own scrawl of a script. I hoped I had not made some error — or if so, that it was not anything significant; but Holmes' visit seemed to belie that wish and covered me with a pall of unease. My mind was awhirl with worry. Perhaps the problem was that I had not let Holmes read the final version of the story before publication? While I knew he was reluctant to read any of my missives of his cases, I realised that offering to show him the manuscript beforehand would have been a wise decision.

'I am sorry, Holmes. Truly, if I have made some error in the Musgrave story . . . '

Holmes shook his head sadly. 'It is not the Musgrave case, old man, but what you added into the story.'

'Added? Whatever do you mean?' I asked, truly perplexed.

'You mentioned my early cases . . . before Musgrave,' he stated flatly.

I thought about that and what I had written about those cases in the story. It had been only the most cursory mention, just a few words or titles here and there. I often did this in my chronicles of his cases, which I felt lent credence with tantalising hints to my stories. He had never said anything about this before. I looked over at him. 'Let me see. I only made mention of the cases you yourself mentioned to me. There was the Tarleton murders, that fellow Vanberry, an old woman — I believe Russian, the aluminium crutch . . . oh yes, and Ricoletti.'

11

'Precisely!' Holmes positively barked out the word.

'Ricoletti?' I asked with a tremor, wondering just what I had done.

Holmes fairly shrieked at me in dismay now. 'Ricoletti of the club foot and his abominable wife!'

'Yes? My God, what is it, Holmes?'

'Ricoletti of the club foot and his abominable wife! Wherever in heaven or hell did you get that, Watson?'

I gulped nervously. 'W-why, from your own words. You mentioned them to me when we looked through your old tin box that day in 1888. I admit you mumbled a bit and my hearing was not quite up to par, but that is what I heard plainly.'

'You heard it plainly?' Holmes shook his head in exasperation.

'Holmes . . . what is it? Please . . . '

Sherlock Holmes stood up to his full height and gave me a piercing look from those hawk-like eyes that froze me in my tracks. Then he sighed and said quite succinctly, 'Watson, that day in 1888, I did *not* say 'Ricoletti of the club foot and his abominable wife' — of all the damnable things; I *said* 'the wrinkled Yeti of the club foot and his abominable life!' Do you see the difference?'

'W-what?' I stammered.

'What, indeed! You have muddled up the facts as never before. It is quite unforgivable. You have created the greatest example of mis-hearing there ever was.'

'Are you sure?' I blurted, dumbfounded, immediately regretting the question.

'Really, Watson, do you ask me if I am sure of my own words?'

'No, of course not.' I swallowed hard, nervous now. 'My God, Holmes, I-I don't know what to say, I am sorry. I had no idea. I feel terrible. My hearing is not as it should be after my experiences in the war, but I swear to you that is what I heard you say that day long ago — or at least that is what I *thought* you said.'

Holmes was not moved.

I pleaded, 'I admit I tend to the melodramatic in my recounting of your cases, but I do try to stick closely to the facts — or the main facts — except in those areas where you have advised me to change names, dates, or certain places. I am so sorry. This is most embarrassing. I do not know what to do about it.'

'Do about it?' Holmes stated sharply. 'You have done quite enough!'

I hung my head down in sad resignation. I had failed my old friend.

Holmes must have felt the truth of my contrition. 'Well, there is nothing you can do about it now. It is all out and in print. It will go down through the ages as one of my earliest unrecorded cases — and it shall remain unpublished.'

'Of course,' I agreed readily.

'Unpublished, but not unrecorded, dear Watson.' Then Sherlock Holmes looked at me with a softness to his features he had not shown yet, obviously taking pity upon the poor wretch I was, and his great heart opened up to me. He shook his head, and then a slim smile escaped his thin lips. 'Really, Watson, you are incorrigible! Ricoletti of the club foot and his abominable wife? Whatever were you thinking? You do need to have your hearing checked.'

I nodded sadly. Then Sherlock Holmes actually laughed, but it was good-natured, and there was a twinkle in his eyes.

'I am sorry,' I said with a deep sigh.

Holmes merely waved his arm in dismissal. 'It is done. There is nothing more we can do about it now.'

I spoke up quickly: 'I can write a retraction, or perhaps a correction, in the next issue of *The Strand*.'

'Yes that would surely do it: bring more attention to the mistake and make yourself look more the fool — and me by implication? No, I think not.'

'Then what can I do to make it up to you, Holmes? I apologise sincerely for this error, and I am terribly embarrassed by it.'

'As you should be, Watson, as you should be,' Holmes chided me, but there was no anger or malice in his voice now. 'However, you do need to make amends.'

'Anything, Holmes!' I stammered eagerly.

'Good; then please bring me a glass of that fine brandy you possess, and I shall tell you the true facts and details behind the strange case of the wrinkled Yeti of the club foot and his abominable life.'

I quickly poured my friend a liberal dose of the liqueur and rushed to gather up my pen and writing pad.

'Take it down, exactly as I give it to you.'

'Of course, Holmes,' I blurted, over-joyed that his anger had abated, and astounded now that he was actually going to recount to me one of his rare early unknown cases. I would make sure to get it right this time.

'Are you ready, Watson?' Holmes asked, taking a sip of the brandy and resting his neck back upon the headset of my large comfortable chair.

I sat across from him upon the settee, prone forward in rapt anticipation with pen and pad in hand.

'Good, then we shall begin.' Holmes then closed his eyes, silent for a moment, obviously his vast mind reaching back through the years collecting and collating the particulars of that early case, gathering every bit of fact and detail like some fantastic thinking machine.

Here, then, is 'The Strange Case of the Wrinkled Yeti of the Club Foot and His Abominable Life' just as Sherlock Holmes told it to me on that warm May morning in 1894.

★ ★ ★

I have a restless mind, Watson; none should know that better than yourself, my old friend. I have always been interested in crime, of course, but that began early on with an interest in puzzles. Also the corollary questions. How do things work? Why do they work the way they do? I also confess an interest in the unusual, the strange — oddities, even freaks. And that is how I came upon the mysterious Yeti. Or, as he is termed by some persons, the Himalayan Monster. But he is called Yeti by the inhabitants of mountainous Nepal, and very much feared. He is a legend, a myth, but one all too real to the people who live there.

The story of it dates back to 1832. The Yeti is said to be a tall beast covered in dark hair walking on two feet, some type of pre-human or prehistoric man perhaps. A missing link? Who can say? Regardless, as an oddity it fascinated me back then in my youth for the simple reason that one of these creatures was said to be on display near London at the time. This was way back in 1878, before the Musgrave Affair, at a time when the Clyde & Barrows Carnival show was in town under a tent outside London on the old fairgrounds.

Well, I had to go and see this wonder for myself. I was young then, and fascinated by such things. At the time there was another such curiosity making all the rage throughout London — that of a horribly deformed young man, Joseph Carey Merrick, or John Merrick to some, who was called by others The Elephant Man. Merrick back then was a mere sixteen-year-old boy, but even then he had massive and rather singular deformities. He earned his living by entertaining customers in what can only be termed a freak show. Merrick proved to be a most charming and shy young man. His 'act' was a rather distasteful display of his

18

horrendous deformities, but through it he was able to earn the money to support himself, afford a small room, and not go hungry. It was a grim Hobson's choice for such a decent young man, but one he was apparently willing to make. I assumed the Yeti at the Clyde & Barrows Carnival would be much the same situation. I was wrong.

On a cool summer morning in 1878, I travelled to the then rural environs outside Greater London where the fairground was located. It was a massive area of some one hundred acres full of gaily coloured tents and painted wagons. It was a circus, gypsy camp, carnival and country fair all rolled into one. It was exciting and also dangerous. Even back then, my criminal senses were well-honed, and I knew the area was home to many a cutpurse, waylayer and scoundrel; but the worst of the lot were not those who preyed upon the unsuspecting thrill-seekers who came there from the city such as myself to spend a few pence and view mysterious oddities and won-ders. The worst of the lot were the men who ran the shows, specifically the sinister and vile exhibits down what was called 'Freak Show Alley'. This was a dark, dreary lane of ratty tents and broken wagons, yelling barkers, smoky rooms, muddy ground, and displays of the most extreme oddities and freaks ever seen — in some cases they crossed the line into utter depravity. There I saw women for sale, children in chains, people kept as cattle, and . . . monsters. I had never seen more debased examples of the human condition. The various 'shows' — a better term would be 'horror shows' — and their masters did all they could to accentuate the ugliness and grotesquerie of their sad exhibitions and to debase their humanity as much as possible. It was in one of these horrid places that my eyes came upon the monstrous Yeti.

I paid my tuppence to a grim ratty fellow at the entrance, and with a large crowd I was quickly ushered into a dark tent where I found myself standing before a large dirt pit. In the pit, in chains and being driven forward to us to view, was the likes of something I had never seen before in my life. It was a man — and yet it was not a man. Could it be one of the fabled Yetis of Nepal, that pre-human creature of the land of snow and ice? I thought not, but it was certainly a reasonable facsimile, and the crowd loved it. They positively ate it up. I watched and began to feel sick. The man — for surely he was a man, and not some Yeti at all — was being horribly mistreated. He looked ill, and he was surely someone of very limited mental abilities. I believe the carnival term is 'geek'. He was quite large, almost seven feet tall, and rather massive, perhaps twenty stone in weight. A veritable monster — but not a monster. And yet his body was all wrinkled and ravaged with deep furrows. It appeared to me that the poor creature was being starved. His head and upper torso were overwhelmed with long matted dark hair; and his body, almost entirely naked but for a small dirty loincloth, was covered in dark hair, along with dirt, mud, bruises, welts and horrible purple blotches. It was obvious the poor wretch had been mercilessly beaten.

21

I stood there, ashamed — ashamed that any human being, no matter how deficient in mental abilities, could be treated in such a horrendous manner. My heart broke for the man, while the crowd roared their delight and approval with every punishment and cruelty the trainer inflicted upon the poor creature. I do not believe they saw him as a human being at all, but the monster he was made out to be. I could only turn away and in disgust walk towards the exit of the tent. I had seen enough. I was severely shaken by what I had viewed, and the roar of approval of the crowd filling my ears made the matter all that much more terrible. As I reached the exit, I felt as if tears would burst forth from my eyes, but instead a deep and pressing anger took hold of me. A rage grew within me.

'I will not allow this to stand!' I barked as I quickly stormed back towards the open pit area. I pushed aside the laughing cheering crowd and walked up to the so-called Yeti beast-man and his malicious trainer. They both looked at me curiously. The 'Yeti' growled fearfully, but I saw no real danger from him, only the fear of the terrified child in his sad eyes. I did not fear any attack from him. The trainer was another matter altogether.

'Wot's this 'ere? Get back, yer bloody fool! We dunna allow any blokes near the mysterious Yeti.' He raised a large club at me threateningly, the same club he used to control the so-called Yeti to beat him into submission.

'I will not let this stand!' I shouted; and before the trainer's club could strike me down, I drove my fist into his face. Blood spurted, he screamed in rage, and then he charged me like a raving bull. I used a useful judo trick I had recently learned to trip him, and when he rose to his feet I gave him another fist to the face. This time the man sank to the muddy floor, unconscious. The crowd roared with delight — they must have thought it all part of the show.

The Yeti shook and swayed back and forth, cried, and sank into a fetal ball. The big terrible monster was just a sad, sick man much abused. I stood there for a moment not knowing quite what to do. I had not planned this out, you see. I had never done such a thing before — it was against my nature to act so impetuously — but I was proud that I had done so. I put it all down now to exuberant youth. Nonetheless, I was at a loss as to what to do next. I saw a commotion brewing at the opening at the far end of the tent. It seemed the trainer's mates were coming inside to see what had happened. They were four burly fellows with clubs, going hard at each person in the tent pushing and knocking them out of the way in an effort to get to me. They would be at me soon. What to do? I quickly approached the Yeti — I call him that for lack of a more accurate word — but he was unable to hear me. I noticed the chain clasped to his ankle. That would surely have to go. I realised the trainer must have the key for the chains; I quickly found it in the man's pocket and released the Yeti.

'You are free! You can leave now!' I stated to the poor man, as the trainer's mates drew closer, carefully inching forward. I had to make my escape soon, or have my head bashed in — for I could not overcome all four attackers. Then I suddenly felt a pull on my sleeve and looked to see one of the most incredible sights I have ever seen in my life.

She was young and quite lovely, but upon her face was a full growth of dark long hair. A beard! A bearded lady!

'Quickly, you have to get out of here, but please help me save John. He doesn't deserve this!'

'John?' I asked quickly.

'The Yeti. Now hurry; my friends will hold off the crew until we can get away.'

Then I saw what she meant. Behind her were a group of the most amazing people I have ever seen. These were the so-called freaks from the various side-shows and tents of Freak Alley. There was a muscle-bound strong man, a very tall and thin 'rubber man', four midgets dressed as police bobbies with of all things night sticks, a fierce 'lion man' with a mane of thick blond hair, and a snake-woman with a very large real snake. I believe it was a python.

'My name is Zelda,' the bearded woman told me.

'Sherlock Holmes,' I replied. It was surely one of my most precarious meetings, under the circumstances.

'Come now, help me get John out of here. We're leaving this place — we've all had enough. A freak show is one thing, but slavery is another matter. Those men held John captive and kept all his money; they treated him terribly because he was so helpless. Now we will take him to safety. Will you help?'

'Of course.'

Zelda turned to her cohort and shouted, 'Here they come. Tear them up, boys!'

The melee that ensued was incredible, but it gave Zelda and me the time we needed to get the Yeti — John — out of the tent and to freedom. I was sure John did not know what was transpiring at all, but he did as Zelda told him to do. It was apparent he trusted her. We led him away as best we could. He had a terribly deformed club foot and he often stumbled, but he did not fall because Zelda and I held him up, one of us at each side of him, as we made our way out.

We escaped through the back of the tent with the mad melee still going on inside. There were screams and running patrons who had never expected such madness at a Freak Alley show. Soon the alley was bursting with terror and chaos. Someone knocked over a wood-burning brazier, and a fire started in one of the tents that soon leapt with the wind and spread to others. Before long, most of Freak Alley was ablaze with roaring flames and screaming, running people. The smoke covered our escape. By then, Zelda and I had taken John to the edge of the fairground, where I was able to procure a wagon and driver to take us to my Montague Street flat back in central London.

Circus people and carny folk look out for each other, and none more so than those possessing the unique talents and abilities that allow them to perform in the freak shows. Zelda and her cohort of fellow entertainers eventually formed their own show in another city, where they continued to exhibit their various

27

talents to earn an honest living. They took good care of the mysterious Yeti — John — who turned out to be one John Anderson, late of the British army and a veteran of the Crimea. It was later learned that John Anderson had been a sergeant of sappers at the Battle of the Alma, where he had exhibited heroic actions. He had been mentioned in dispatches, but was presumed lost in action. His club foot was the result of a broken foot in that battle that had never been set or healed properly. However, far worse than his physical wounds were his mental ones. He had lost his mind in the battle. John was later found on the battlefield and brought back to England, and then quickly discharged where he became just another beggar on the streets of London. He had allowed himself to grow unkempt and dirty, with long matted hair and apparent mindless actions. That was when his 'trainer' found him, and in a brilliant blaze of morbid inspiration took him captive and created the Monstrous Yeti.

Now John Anderson was free. Many

years later, I heard tell of how he still thrilled the people of a northern city with his antics. Zelda and her troupe of entertainers took good care of him. He peacefully passed away in his sleep in late 1895. And that, my good Watson, is the true story of 'The Wrinkled Yeti of the Club Foot and His Abominable Life'.

*　*　*

Sherlock Holmes smiled at me and said, 'And now, I believe I'll take another glass of that excellent brandy, if you please.'

'Of course.' I jumped up to pour him one more full glass, as I thought about all he had just told me. I looked at him expectantly. 'An amazing story, Holmes. Simply amazing! Thank you for relating it to me, and for setting the record straight.'

'I have always told you, Watson, that you often play fast and loose with the facts; but this time it was an error of gigantic proportions even for you. We are lucky there is no one but us who knows the truth behind your mistake. However, I do want you to do something for me now.

You have written up this story just as I have told it to you, and now I want you to hide it away. Then someday, perhaps after our deaths, it will be discovered by some lucky soul and the true story of the case can then be told. We need to set this right, but it need not be set right in our lifetimes. I fear it would make us both look the fool otherwise.'

'Of course, Holmes. I will do whatever you wish.' Then I took the pad that contained my manuscript of the story written exactly as Holmes had told it to me, and folded it into a tight little bundle and wrapped it inside a waterproof package. I looked over at Holmes, he indicated the desk in the corner.

'That is my wife's desk, not mine,' I explained.

Holmes only nodded with a slight smile. 'Better yet — or perhaps, better *Yeti*, eh, Watson?'

I nodded. Though he was not usually given to puns, it did show me a change for the better in my friend's disposition. I placed the manuscript package in the top desk drawer.

'No, Watson, take out the drawer. In the back of the opening you will find a small ledge. After I leave you, take a hammer and small nails and affix it there. Then replace the drawer. Do not tell your wife, and we will erase this embarrassing matter from our minds forever. We will speak of it no more. Perhaps a hundred years from now, some sly fellow will come upon your hidden manuscript. I only hope he knows what to make of it.'

'Thank you, Holmes.'

'Good old Watson. I must say this turned out to be a pleasant visit after all.'

'Always good to see you, Holmes.'

'And I you, Watson.'

Then Sherlock Holmes left my home on his way back to the rooms that held so many memories for both of us, 221B Baker Street.

Before I affixed the manuscript package which I have now entitled 'The Strange Case of the Wrinkled Yeti of the Club Foot and His Abominable Life', I added some additional introductory paragraphs, as well as this brief addendum of explanation to the lucky fellow who may someday find this package. It is upon you now to see to it that my embarrassing error is corrected in the popular press and all is set right for eternity in this matter as per the wishes of my friend, the great detective, Sherlock Holmes.

Yours most truly,

John H. Watson, M.D., late of the British army.

HISTORICAL NOTE:

One of the most intriguing hints of an unrecorded Sherlock Holmes case given to us by Watson in the canon is the snippet, 'Ricoletti of the club foot and his abominable wife'. What did it mean? What was it about? Watson and Holmes give us no facts, no details, just that brief phrase as a hint. However, that intriguing passage has become fodder for much speculation by Sherlockians over the decades. It is estimated that there have been no less than 17 published written records of this case by various authors in various pastiches. Unfortunately, all of them have proven wrong, until now. In his book *A Sherlock Holmes Commentary*

(David & Charles, UK, 1972), D. Martin Dakin on page 113 talks about how Watson misheard Holmes' words about the matter; after all, he never saw the phrase written down, so the good doctor got it wrong when he mentioned this case in his retelling of 'The Musgrave Ritual'. Well, it wouldn't be the first time! Regarding The Himalayan Monster, also known as the Yeti, it would not be called The Abominable Snowman until 1921, when that term was first coined.

Happy Birthday, Mr. Holmes!

It was in late 1903, after the affair I would eventually chronicle as 'The Adventure of the Creeping Man' for *The Strand* magazine, when my friend Sherlock Holmes seemed to be in an unusual mood of dark disturbance. I could only assume that it was the Abercrombie situation that was playing upon his mind — a dangerous escaped convict who was said to be on his way to London. Holmes would not speak of it, and even the press was sparse regarding details, so I put the matter aside for the time being. I had concerns of my own just then causing me considerable consternation.

Mary, my wife, had gone away for a protracted visit to the north country to look after her ailing mother, so I found myself alone and lonely at home without her. I was much buoyed when Holmes suggested I move back into our old lodgings at Baker Street for the next month or two while she was away. It was a generous offer on his part to assuage my loneliness, and I felt beholden to do something to reciprocate his generosity — and I knew exactly what I would do to repay my good friend.

'Watson? Now what is it?' Sherlock Holmes asked me with obvious disdain that morning as we finished breakfast. 'I can smell the wood burning.'

'Should I stoke down the fire?' I asked coyly.

'Hah! Not the fireplace, old man, but you, your very thoughts. Your mind is working in high gear. I fear you may hurt yourself if you tax your faculties so harshly.'

'You . . . fear . . . what?' I blurted, holding down my chagrin.

Holmes laughed, allowing a mischievous grin. 'You are up to something. I can read the signs all over you, though you are trying hard to hide it. Now I wonder what it can be?'

'Really, Holmes! You can be insufferable at times.'

Sherlock Holmes smiled victoriously, I knew he was playing with me now. 'That does it! Now whatever can you be planning? Surely not that execrable birthday party scheme again? Each year at this time you endeavour to harass me with that ridiculous nonsense, and each year I refuse you adamantly.'

'That may be, Holmes, but this is different. This January the sixth will be your fiftieth birthday, a singular milestone in your life and career.' I spoke softly, imploringly, for I knew his rages and upon this matter he had always been very firm. Nevertheless, I felt I had to press ahead; for he was correct, you see: I did have plans. I added, 'This is a special moment in your life. You should celebrate this occasion. I wish to celebrate it. Many people would like to celebrate it with you.'

'Then do so. Tip a pint! Tip a dozen pints for all I care, but do please leave me out of it. I have no wish to be put on display, regaled by gawkers with whom I am forced to make pleasantries, while being force-fed food and victuals, then stuffed with cake or pastry, only to finally be presented with meaningless gifts — none of which I need by the way — all the time having to thank the givers profusely! I can think of nothing more demeaning or loathsome. Why, I should be forced to resort to the cocaine needle, or even the opium pipe, to assuage my wounded psyche. Thank you, but no thank you, Watson.'

'But, Holmes . . . ?' I stammered, then stopped abruptly, for I saw his face had grown dark and grim.

My companion only shook his head sadly and suddenly flung down his *Times*, then he swiftly arose from his chair with a huff and marched into his bedroom, slamming the door firmly behind him. I believe Holmes had made known his feelings quite clear to me upon the subject of birthdays, but I would not let that stop me from planning a party in his honour — whether he wanted one or not!

★　★　★

The next day, Holmes and I were in our sitting room. He was smoking prodigiously upon his favourite pipe, creating quite the thick fog, no doubt deep in some deductive thoughts. I was quietly perusing my notes of the Carfax Case.

'Holmes?' I inquired softly.

He looked up at me and allowed a grim smile. 'Absolutely not, Watson!'

'But . . . but . . . '

'No 'buts' need be applied. I know you are ignoring my wishes and are planning to have a birthday party for me here on January the sixth. I know you will invite friends and even some . . . acquaintances.'

'Please, Holmes, be reasonable.'

'Reasonable, Watson! You harm me deeply with this request. I want no party. I have never wanted a party. I never celebrate my date of birth. A ridiculous custom. Why should I begin now? In any event, do as you will, but I certainly will never attend such a gathering. Case closed.'

I nodded, subdued by my friend's firm conviction but more determined than ever to give him a party to celebrate his life, something he so richly deserved. 'Your birthday party will go on with or without you, Holmes,' I stated firmly.

'Then it shall go on without me,' he replied just as firmly. I could see he was immovable upon this subject, so I would have to amend my plans accordingly. My ace in the hole was his brother, Mycroft, who told me that at the right time he would call Holmes away upon some pretext.

* * *

The days passed, and Holmes seemed distracted by several interesting cases that climaxed at the end of the year of 1903. The situation regarding Abercrombie I could tell was now uppermost in his mind, but he would still give me no details.

New Year's Day, 1904 saw us enjoying a lovely dinner compliments of our landlady, Mrs. Hudson. She winked at me as she took away the empty dishes of our feast. She was excited by the idea of the party, now merely a few days away, and naturally the first person after Mycroft that I had invited. She was overjoyed by the idea but had not let on to Holmes her excitement. I believe she was more difficult for Holmes to read than was I. Irrespective of all that, I began to grow concerned because the big event was now just five days away.

Holmes remained as obdurate as ever upon the subject. 'So, my good Watson, you thought your little plan slipped my mind in all the rush of recent cases. I assure you, nothing could be further from the truth.'

'Be reasonable, Holmes,' I implored once more, trying to take a different tack with him.

'Reasonable? Yes, by all means, I shall be. My reasonableness extends to the promise that I shall not leave here the entire day of the sixth. Ah, but do not celebrate victory just yet, my friend. For I will allow no visitors to enter our rooms either. Nor will I permit you to hang one single party ribbon or atrocious piece of celebratory bunting anywhere on these premises. If you do so, I will simply pull them down and tear them into tiny pieces. So you see, my friend, your party is effectively aborted. It shall be stillborn. Now why not just admit defeat so we can put all this silliness behind us? There is a new magic act at the *Lyceum* that is all the rage, a female magician by the name of 'The Young and Lovely Lucille', and I have obtained two tickets. What do you say?'

'So that is how you prove to be reasonable? To buy me off! I am sorry, my friend, but I do not accept your offer. January the sixth marks your half-century, and upon my soul, a celebration of your birth will take place upon that day!'

Holmes just moaned, relit his pipe and walked over to our front window to stare down at Baker Street below. I saw him take something from his pocket, look over it carefully, then quickly put it back into his pocket. Was it the tickets, or something else? I had no idea what it was about, but he looked grim now. Holmes was quiet and in deep thought and grew morose, as if struggling with something, but he would not tell me, and I knew better than to ask. I knew with my friend that all things were made known in their proper time, so I did not intrude upon his thoughts. Since my marriage and moving out of Baker Street, I feared he had gone back to his old secretive ways. He was being difficult. Nevertheless, I did not care, Sherlock Holmes was going to have his birthday party if it was the last thing I ever did — but he had now put up a serious impediment to my plan.

★   ★   ★

When the morning of the sixth approached, I felt that all was lost. Holmes was firmly ensconced in our rooms like some grim stone monument, unmoving, inflexible. True to his word, he would allow no visitors, not even Mrs. Hudson. He would not allow me to decorate the rooms. I was effectively flummoxed. I had the nightmare thought of Holmes standing steadfastly behind our locked door all that evening, chiding our guests by not allowing them to enter. Some of the people I had invited were coming from quite a distance. It was looking as if all my plans would end up in utter disaster.

Of course Mycroft was essential to my plans, but upon the morning of the party his scheme to get Sherlock out of our rooms upon some pretext proved futile. Holmes would not bite. He would not take the bait Mycroft dangled before him. What was I to do? And guests would be arriving later that very evening, just hours away.

As the day wore on, my nerves grew more frayed. Holmes just sat there calmly smoking up a storm, a whimsical smile playing across his face as he watched me squirm in my agitated state of quiet dismay. I quite believe he was enjoying my distress. The scoundrel!

The morning passed badly. Later, Mrs. Hudson brought us up a light luncheon. Holmes graciously allowed her to enter our rooms and she quietly placed the meal tray down before us. She shot me an inquiring look, and when Holmes was distracted her lips made the silent words, 'What is happening?' I shook my head negatively. Nothing was happening. I could well understand her concern, but I was nonplussed by Holmes' activity — or lack of it. He was still determined not to leave our rooms, and I realised that by doing so, he had effectively stymied all my party plans.

I had to get Holmes out of our rooms so I could decorate them, then bring up the food and punch that Mrs. Hudson had secreted below, and I had to do this all before our guests arrived. Then, even more difficult — I had to somehow get Holmes to come back to 221B. That was the real rub — but I would worry about that later, as I was looking to Mycroft to help me with that obstacle.

After a quiet lunch, the early afternoon was too soon upon us and I was simply jittery with nerves, though trying hard not to let it show. I did not want to give Holmes the satisfaction. For his part, my friend continued smoking and watched me with a rather whimsical leer upon his face. He was quite enjoying my discomfiture and openly taunted me with quick jibes, inquiring how the party was shaping up, and if all was in readiness, reminding me that time was growing short.

'You can be abominable sometimes,' I stated, anger covering my hurt pride.

Holmes just sat there glowing in my distress. He even had the effrontery to ask, 'Do you need any help decorating?'

'No, thank you!' I barked, quite upset now that he was obviously doing all he could to make me squirm. He was baiting me. Well, I would have none of it, but I forced myself to calm down. I took a deep breath, sighed and asked, 'Holmes?'

'No, Watson, not at all,' he stated firmly; but then I was surprised to see him get up from his chair, walk over to the door and put on his coat. Now what? I thought.

'I think I need to get a bit of fresh air,' Holmes suddenly informed me in a firm tone. 'The air in here is a bit stuffy. I believe I will go out for a walk. I shan't return before the early morning of the seventh, Watson, so have your party if you must, but know that I shall not be in attendance.'

Then Sherlock Holmes left our rooms

and was soon gone. I ran over to the front window and saw him walking briskly down Baker Street. I sighed and gathered myself together, astounded by this sudden action but overjoyed, for this was just the break I had hoped for. I immediately called down to our landlady that we were to begin to set the party in motion.

'Mrs. Hudson, he's gone out, the party is on! Full speed ahead!'

'Jolly good, Doctor Watson! Jolly good!'

Mrs. Hudson proved a bounty of excellent ideas. First she helped me move the chairs and sofa out of our sitting room and into Holmes' bedroom to create more open space. My bedroom would be used for the hats and coats of our guests. Then we moved our breakfast table in front of the fireplace, which created a large open area for guests to mingle. Soon afterwards our landlady brought up plate after plate of enticing finger sandwiches along with her famous rum punch. The guests began to arrive promptly at the prearranged hour of seven o'clock.

Inspector Lestrade of Scotland Yard

was the first on the scene, accompanied by Inspector Tobias Gregson. They were old friends who had known Holmes for almost twenty years, since the case I had chronicled as 'A Study in Scarlet' back in '87. Also from Scotland Yard were Inspectors Stanley Hopkins and the younger Alec MacDonald, who Holmes felt showed great promise and referred to as 'Mr. Mac'. While it was good to see them all, I thought it a bit odd, since my invitation had only gone out to Lestrade. Now there seemed to be many more men of the law arriving than I had originally invited, and I barely knew what to do about it. I finally shrugged and accepted it in good order, putting it down to Holmes' long years of work with the police.

Then Wiggins and his small gang of former street ruffians appeared, whom Holmes liked to call his Baker Street Irregulars. Various others entered the house and our rooms: former clients; people with whom Holmes had come into contact with over the years. There were so many. It was good to see Holmes' old friend from Oxford, Reginald Musgrave, once again, whose strange problem I had written up as 'The Musgrave Ritual' so many years ago; as well as my old friend 'Young' Stamford, quite older now and a distinguished medical man. Stamford was the fellow who had first introduced me to Holmes so many years before. Mycroft Holmes appeared soon afterwards. I was happy to see him, and to see that tonight's party was important enough for him to uproot himself from his sedentary seat in the Diogenes Club.

'Is Sherlock here yet?' the elder Holmes brother asked me; he was Sherlock's senior by seven years. He immediately turned towards the refreshments table and liberally partook of Mrs. Hudson's exquisite rum punch, which was proving to be the hit of the evening. Soon the room filled with still more guests, all of whom were talking softly in little clusters, all seemingly sharing their favourite Sherlock Holmes story or memory. I felt sad that the great man himself would not be here for any of this celebration and that he would miss it all. It was a shame.

'I'm afraid your brother will not be coming,' I told Mycroft Holmes glumly.

I looked around the rooms. They were nicely decorated; Mrs. Hudson and I had done a credible job. The party was going full force, with even our bedrooms and the outer landing and stairway filling up with happily chatting guests.

'Oh, I think not, Doctor Watson,' Mycroft told me with a little smile. 'I am sure brother Sherlock could never resist such an event, all his protestations aside. However, you may be correct; he certainly is not the birthday type.'

'I know that only too well,' I blurted, my eyes scanning through the rooms and into the outer landing. Something did not seem right. There seemed to be many more guests than I had ever invited. Though I scanned every face visible to me, I did not see my friend at all. I looked enquiringly at the elder Holmes. 'I do not see Sherlock anywhere,' I stated.

Mycroft smiled indulgently. 'Perhaps he is in disguise?'

'Disguise? Of course!' Yes, that had to be it! The wily scoundrel was in disguise.

I knew Holmes' massive ego could not allow him to resist being present at his own party so that he could investigate all the goings-on — but it never occurred to me that he would do so in disguise. I simply assumed he would arrive later, as would any other person, when the party was going full throttle, and make some grand entrance. It never occurred to me that he might already be here, right this very minute.

I looked over all the faces once again. I quickly discounted the Scotland Yard inspectors and others I knew by sight, but there was a problem: there seemed to be an alarming number of guests whom I did not know at all. Men, and even women, I had never seen before. That was perplexing. Who were all these people? Where had they all come from? There were also a number of rather flirtatious women present. What were they doing here? I was confused. I had planned for a rather small gathering, an intimate party, not this! It was rapidly turning into a three-ring circus. Holmes' great popularity had apparently grown beyond even my own comprehension.

'Can you tell me which of these men is your brother?' I asked Mycroft hopefully.

'No, Doctor, I do not see him here,' Mycroft replied with a wry grin.

'Then how do I find him?' I asked hopelessly.

'If he is here at all, you must use the deductive methods you have learned from my brother. If you do so, I am certain you cannot go wrong, Dr. Watson.' Then Mycroft Holmes walked off with a glass of rum punch to speak to someone who appeared to be a member of the royal family, who was speaking to a man I knew to be the French ambassador.

Now I was in a quandary. Holmes had apparently secretly stolen into his own birthday party without my knowledge, and perhaps was here in disguise, but I could not find him. I was sure the fiend was doing this just to annoy me. I feared he might not ever reveal himself, which would certainly put a damper upon the party. It was all up to me now.

Once again my eyes looked over each of the guests. There were quite a lot of them. I certainly had not invited them all, for I did not even know them. Some certainly appeared to be rather disreputable examples of the lower, or even criminal, classes. I wondered how many might be burglars, forgers, pickpockets or confidence men. I was aghast. I even recognised one man Holmes had been instrumental in having arrested, wily Jack Thomas the pocket-picker. He, at least, was harmless. I sighed, shaking my head in wonder. What was going on here? Then I saw another man who seemed familiar to me. I assumed he was one of the reformed criminals who sometimes aided Holmes. Maybe he knew something. I sidled up to him.

'Glad you could make Mr. Holmes' party,' I stated. Then I introduced myself, saying, 'Dr. John Watson.'

'I knows who you be; I seen you with Mr. 'Olmes 'pon occasion. I helps him sometimes. Me name be Rafferty.'

'Rafferty? Just Rafferty?'

'Rafferty will do for today, eh?' he responded with a snicker, showing a mouth full of blackened teeth. Wherever

Holmes had met such a disreputable rogue, I feared to imagine.

'Well, Mr. Rafferty . . . '

'No, sir, just Rafferty,' he corrected me, quite adamant upon the matter. He showed me a fierce demeanor and I grew nervous.

I took a step back, wondering if I might not need my revolver before this evening was over. Had this man come here to . . . burgle the house? No, my alarm was unnecessary; he was a reformed criminal who had told me he now worked with my companion, so he should prove safe. At least I hoped so. However, as I looked around the room at all the unknown faces, it dawned upon me that there were many people who wished to do harm to my friend, and one of them might even be here at this very party. The thought chilled me.

I decided to put this Rafferty fellow to the test. 'So you have done some work for Mr. Holmes?' I asked, looking at him closely, eye to eye.

'That I does, 'pon occasion, as it warrants.'

'Then perhaps you can help me?'

'If I am able, depending 'pon what it be.'

I nodded, then I drew the man in close to me and whispered in his ear, 'Listen, Sherlock Holmes is here, but he is in disguise. Can you point him out to me?'

'That is not for me to say. If Mr. 'Olmes desires not to be known, he should remain so. He may be working on one of those cases of his,' Rafferty explained in a conspiratorial whisper.

I'm afraid I grew exasperated by his defiance, and showed it. 'Oh come now, my man — this is a birthday party; Holmes is not working on any case. He is just trying to get my goat and punish me for giving him a party that he never wanted.'

The man shrugged and then left me to converse with one of the young ladies present. Now who these ladies were, I had no idea. I noticed all were rather comely, and if truth be told, well-endowed and quite fetching. I shook my head in despair and forgot them. I was a married man now, my Mary was away, and my friend

Sherlock Holmes was doing his best to make me out a fool. Soon each of the guests was coming over to me and asking when Sherlock Holmes would appear. When indeed! I was in a quandary.

'Any luck yet?' Mycroft asked as he passed me with someone who looked like the prime minister.

'No, but who are all these people? I am sure I invited no more than two dozen guests, but I have discovered people all throughout our rooms, out on the landing, the stairway, down through Mrs. Hudson's entire first floor, and even outside in front of 221. What is going on here?'

'My brother, your friend, is quite the popular fellow,' Mycroft answered with a jolly laugh. Then he left to refill his glass with more rum punch. I watched him walk off and shook my head in despair. I was in a real dilemma.

Gregson and Lestrade next walked over to me. 'When will Mr. Holmes arrive?' asked the former.

'Soon,' I answered, then begged off, telling them that I had to speak with another guest on the other side of the room.

It was then that my eyes locked onto the elderly clergyman. He was tall and lean, with long grey hair under a large black slough hat. He carried a book with him under his arm. Probably a Bible. He was talking briskly with one of the ladies. Now here was someone of interest. Hello! Holmes had once used this very disguise years ago in the Adler affair. I looked more closely at the old cleric. Yes, it made sense. This could certainly be Holmes. My heart leapt with joy. I had him now! I would show him!

I watched the old clergyman more carefully. Yes, it could certainly be Holmes — in fact, it *had* to be Holmes! I looked around for Mycroft to tell him, but he was nowhere in sight, so I decided to beard this Sherlock myself. I approached the elderly clergyman and stood boldly in front of him. I stared him down. He looked back at me as if he had never seen me before, just as I assumed he would.

I said boldly, 'Holmes, I must compliment you upon your fine disguise: the old weathered face, the lank messy hair, the crazed look in the eyes. But I saw right through it immediately. I have found you out, you scoundrel!'

The old cleric looked at me uncomprehendingly, and it annoyed me that my friend would not admit defeat and insisted upon keeping up his sham in spite of my discovering his charade. With some annoyance the cleric said, 'Disguise? What disguise, young man? I am sorry, sir, but I quite do not know what you mean.'

'You old rascal! Come now, admit I found you out!' I said rather loudly, insisting he come clean with the truth, sure that I had breached his disguise. We were attracting a crowd.

'Come now, sir. Doctor Watson, is it not? This is most unusual.'

'You know who *I* am, and I know who *you* are, you wily rogue, you!'

'Well, this is very unseemly behaviour. I have been invited here for a party to celebrate Mr. Holmes' auspicious day, and now I find myself verbally accosted by some loud-mouthed mountebank!

This is nothing short of outrageous!'

'*Mountebank!* Why you old faker, I'll show you!' I blurted in anger. A crowd had definitely gathered around us now. I saw the men from Scotland Yard, I saw that Rafferty fellow, I saw a tall overweight man who appeared to be a common labourer, another man in a military uniform, Wiggins and Mrs. Hudson — all were looking to see what I would do next.

'Answer me, Holmes! I've had quite enough of your obtuse behaviour, making a fool out of me by coming in secret to your own party and calling *me* a mountebank!'

'Mountebank is the least of it! You are an impertinent scoundrel, sir!' the old cleric barked in anger. 'And a deranged lunatic!'

'Oh, be quiet, Holmes!' I shouted. 'I am furious with you. Why, it would serve you right if I just pulled that fake beard right off your face!'

The elderly cleric took a step back, and I took a step forward, but then I felt a firm hand upon my shoulder. I turned to

58

find Mycroft Holmes standing beside me. He bowed down and gently whispered into my ear, 'I'm afraid you have the wrong man, Doctor. That is the Reverend Mathias James of St. Catherine's. I invited him here myself. You see, my brother did some little favour for him regarding the pilfering of the church's poor box last month. He only wished to express his gratitude.'

My face turned ashen; it must have, because I was so utterly embarrassed. I could barely stand there in front of all those people. Thankfully by then the crowd had moved off and the general party conversation resumed. I well imagined I was the subject of much of that conversation. I took a deep breath and looked to the elder Holmes.

'Not Sherlock?' I asked in a deflated tone.

'Indeed not,' Mycroft replied firmly. Then he pulled me away with him. 'Come, Doctor, you need some of this exquisite rum punch; your nerves seem frayed. Too much excitement for one evening, I gather. The party is simply smashing, by the way — a very interesting group, and they all seem to be having a fine time of things. You are to be congratulated.'

I walked off, numbly following Mycroft, my mind in a whirl. That poor old reverend. I would have to apologise to him later. My God, I had come one heartbeat away from pulling his beard whiskers right out of his face!

'By the way, Doctor, do you have any idea when my brother will show himself?' the elder Holmes asked me confidentially.

I looked at him curiously. 'What do you mean? I thought you said he was here, but in disguise?'

'I said he *might* be here, *perhaps* in disguise,' Mycroft told me.

'So he is not here?'

'Apparently he is not,' Mycroft replied simply.

I felt deflated, defeated, and suddenly very sad. Mycroft handed me a glass of rum punch. I grasped it eagerly and drank four long swallows that emptied the glass. The warmth of the rum and the sweetness of the fruit punch did much to restore my spirits. 'What now?' I asked.

'Be patient,' Mycroft said, and then he walked off to speak with the tall uniformed military man I had seen earlier.

I quickly took another glass of rum punch; my nerves were frazzled and I needed the drink. I'd not only made a fool of myself in front of everyone, I'd practically scared the daylights out of poor old Reverend James. He must think me quite insane. This party was certainly not turning out as I had planned.

As the night wore on, the talk became louder, the laughter more raucous, and no one left 221B. Everyone, it seemed, was waiting for Sherlock Holmes to make his grand entrance to celebrate his fiftieth birthday. No one was more anxious for that event to occur than I.

I decided to make the rounds; and after a few more doses of Mrs. Hudson's delightful elixir — she seemed to keep the punch bowl and trays of food endlessly supplied — I loosened up somewhat and spoke to some of the guests. I focused especially on those whom I did not know.

There were quite a few of them; men of apparently all backgrounds and stations in life. I introduced myself to them all, looking to see if any of them might be Holmes in disguise. I was much more careful this time. Yet while it seemed that none of them could be Holmes, each one asked me when the guest of honour was slated to appear. I smiled and mumbled something about him having been called away earlier in the day on some important business, but that he would surely be here soon.

'Rest assured,' I told one and all with a rum-punch grin, 'Sherlock Holmes would never miss his own birthday party.'

They all laughed and said that was certainly true. I laughed with them as I walked away. I was a desperate man now. What to do? Where was Holmes? Why was he doing this to me?

Someone was tugging at my sleeve. 'Excuse me, Doctor Watson, but can you tell me when Mr. Holmes is going to show up? You know the hour is getting rather late.'

The same question was put to me by

an ever-growing number of guests until it became a veritable chant. 'Where is Holmes? Where is Holmes?'

I swallowed hard and took a deep breath. It looked like I would have to do something soon. But what? It was obvious to me now that Holmes was not going to show up — and if by some miracle he was even here, he was not going to show himself. It looked like it had fallen to me to do the best I could as matters now stood.

I took another deep breath and marshalled my thoughts. Speaking in my best booming voice, I announced to the congregation: 'My friends, ladies and gentlemen, friends of Sherlock Holmes — the hour is getting late. I am afraid to tell you that Holmes is away on a case and will not be able to join us this evening, so we should have our cake now and then call it a night.' There were the expected murmurs of shock and disappointment. 'I am truly sorry that Mr. Holmes is not able to be with us tonight, but he sends his regrets and warmest regards, and he thanks you all for doing him such an honour on his birthday. I am sorry that I have let you down.'

There were more murmurs of disappointment, and some signs of regret. My announcement about Holmes had spread a pall over the formerly joyous party. Now a hush had overcome the guests, joined by a low murmur as they all looked towards me, some not too kindly. I realised something more was called for.

I boldly moved to the front of the room, looked at the guests, and spoke the only way I knew how — from my heart. 'My friends, my good friends, honoured guests — we have joined here tonight to celebrate the fiftieth year after the birth of our good friend Sherlock Holmes. It is fitting we do this. It matters not that Holmes is unable to join us. Holmes is a man who has touched all our lives, and in that way he is with us always. He is a man who has made the world a better place; and without him and his work as a consulting detective, we would all be worse off. I know I would be.

'On a personal note, Sherlock Holmes is my very dear friend. He is the most decent man I have ever met. My life without him would be lost. I miss him being here tonight as much as you all do. I am sure the only reason he is not here with us tonight is because he is engaged in important work that may be a matter of life and death. You can rest assured that once I see him, I shall chide him without mercy for his absence!'

There was a bit of light laughter from the guests at that remark, and I smiled, knowing that I was winning over the crowd. Then I continued: 'What I do know is that were Sherlock Holmes here, he would be overcome by this outpouring of love and affection that you all show him. So many old friends are here together again, and all to honour him. Holmes would be deeply touched, and thank you all.'

There was a cheer, and then clapping, and I quickly wiped away the nervous sweat that streamed down my face. 'I think it is time — let's have our cake!' I announced to raucous cheers. 'Mrs. Hudson!'

By then, of course, everyone was

swarming around me, each one wishing Holmes good cheer and congratulations: Lestrade, Gregson and all the Scotland Yard inspectors; Wiggins and his gang; Stamford; Reginald Musgrave; various clients; and even some men Holmes had put away — all offered their good wishes. I even noticed another Stamford offer his congratulations, Archie Stamford the forger, and then Mycroft stepped up and shook my hand.

'Well done, Doctor Watson, well done indeed!' the elder Holmes told me, and I beamed with pride.

Then the crowd suddenly parted as a familiar female voice called out boldly in a loud Scottish accent: 'Come on now, move off, make room! Comin' through!'

It was Mrs. Hudson holding a large chocolate cake set ablaze with candles — fifty of them if I am not mistaken. She deftly placed the cake down upon the table in front of us.

'Seeing as Mr. Holmes is not present, Doctor Watson, why don't you make a wish for him and then blow out the candles,' she stated. Then she ordered,

'Hurry up or the cake will melt, and everyone is waiting for a piece.'

I took a minute to look around at all the faces beaming with good cheer, and I do believe my eyes misted up for just a moment. In that instant I missed Holmes greatly, so sorry he was missing this celebration in his honour. Then I quickly took a deep breath and blew out all the candles in one great gust of wind.

Instantly those in the room, and all those throughout the entire house, let out with a raucous chant of:

For he's a jolly good fellow!
For he's a jolly good fellow!
For he's a jolly good fellow,
Which nobody can deny!
Happy birthday, Mr. Holmes!

I was obviously touched by the emotion exhibited for my friend and simply said, 'Thank you all — Sherlock Holmes thanks you all!' Then Mrs. Hudson cut the cake and began handing it out to the guests on her prized china.

Wiggins then came over to me on the

sly. He was the one who put me on the right track. 'Eh, Doctor Watson, you 'ear from Mr. 'Olmes yet?'

'You know I haven't, you rascal,' I replied, a bit short with the young man. I'd known Wiggins since he had been a young pup, just a boy — one of those Holmes liked to call his 'irregulars'.

'Well, 'e told me you should be on the lookout for Abercrombie,' Wiggins said in a low tone.

'You spoke with Holmes? Where is he?' I asked quietly. 'Point him out to me now!'

'I can't; 'e told me this yesterday, and I've not seen nor 'eard from 'im since.'

'Abercrombie?' I said softly. That meant something. The escaped convict. Here! What was that about? I looked at Wiggins. 'Did he tell you what this Abercrombie looked like, or why I should be on the watch for him?'

'No, sir; just that you should keep your eyes open and stay away from him.'

I shook my head in frustration. How could I look out for this Abercrombie, or stay away from him, when I did not even know what the man looked like? And a dangerous escaped convict at that! Here? Then my eyes spotted the Scotland Yard inspectors talking heatedly in a small circle apparently about old cases, and having a fine time of it — Lestrade, Gregson, Hopkins, and Mr. Mac.

I smiled as I entered their midst, 'Gentlemen!'

'Fine party, Doctor Watson,' Lestrade said as he downed more punch and picked up another sandwich.

'Simply smashing!' Hopkins added with a grin. It appeared the rum punch had already had some effect upon him — as it was having on most of the guests.

'Gentlemen, perhaps you can help me?' I asked cordially. 'Have any of you heard of the escaped convict, Abercrombie?'

'Dangerous man,' Mr. Mac stated seriously.

'Murderer with no pity,' Gregson added.

I gulped nervously. Those were not the words I wanted to hear, but I expected no less. 'Do any of you know what he looks like? Could you pick him out in a crowd?'

I asked hopefully.

All four inspectors looked dubious and shook their heads in the negative. Hopkins then explained, 'Abercrombie has always appeared the same: shaved round head, clean-shaved face, even his eyebrows are shaved. He's been on the run for over a month — ample time to change his appearance — so unless you see a man matching that description, you'll never find him. He's probably on a ship to America or Australia at this very moment.'

'I hope so,' I said.

Then they asked about my interest in him. I shrugged and just replied that I had read of him in the press and it was a passing fancy.

I next tried Mycroft, but he was also of no help. I found myself back where I had started. I looked over at the many men in the room, then thought of all the other men throughout the house. I knew that there could easily be a dozen or more who might be Abercrombie. Which one was he? Abercrombie the escaped convict! Why was he here? I nodded, now

70

convinced there could be but one reason. Abercrombie was here to kill Sherlock Holmes!

A deadly chill ran through me at the realisation. There really was much more to this party than met the eye; and if Holmes was truly here, I now hoped he *was* in disguise and would *not* reveal himself.

I walked through the rooms and the outer landing, down the stairs, and even to the outside steps of 221 for any sign of Holmes — or a man who might be my friend in disguise. There was no one. Where was he? And this Abercrombie! What of him? Obviously the two were stalking each other in some mad dance of criminal pursuit and revenge. I began to fear for my friend, and told my feelings to Mycroft.

'I feel terrible,' I said to the elder Holmes. 'I never thought that Sherlock taking on a disguise might be for some other reason — that it was a matter of life and death.'

'Fear not, good Doctor. Sherlock has all well in hand.'

'Where is he, then?' I asked nervously.

'I think it may be time. Did you notice the military officer in the red uniform?' Mycroft asked me, a slight smile playing across his lips.

'Sherlock?' I whispered softly.

Mycroft did not answer that question. Instead he told me: 'He is Colonel Sir Ralph Richards. As I say, an interesting fellow. Perhaps you would like me to introduce you to him?'

I nodded. Being a retired army doctor, I was always eager to meet another military man. Mycroft took me to where the colonel was apparently holding court. He was busy speaking with various guests, including Reverend James, that Rafferty fellow, and a disreputable man who appeared to be some sort of overweight common labourer. What *he* was doing here I could not fathom. The man appeared to be nothing more than some heavy oaf, a down-and-out ne'er-do-well who had apparently crashed the party for the free food and beverages supplied so amply by Mrs. Hudson. I watched with astonishment as he wolfed down food and drink like he had never seen such victuals before. Well, so be it. The poor fellow was apparently hungry, and welcome to it. I quickly turned away from the man to look at the other guests.

In a voice loud enough for all to hear, Mycroft Holmes said, 'Colonel Sir Ralph Richards, I would like to present to you a good friend of my brother's, and our host for the evening, Doctor John H. Watson.'

The colonel and I shook hands and exchanged pleasantries. I looked carefully at this military man and was perplexed. Now, *he* could be Holmes in disguise. He was tall and lean, but the uniform covered much. The cap and longish black hair, the large moustache and mutton-chop whiskers, all seemed to disguise him quite well. *If* it was Holmes. I was not quite sure, especially after my previous run-in with the Reverend James, who was nearby and watching me closely as if I were some escapee from Bedlam. I saw him take a careful step back from me and sighed.

I was considering the possibility that the colonel might just be Holmes in disguise when that party-crashing oaf, apparently fully drunk and now disorderly to boot, lost his balance and bumped me hard, pushing me with a wild fall into Rafferty. There was a tussle, a confusion of arms and legs. I tried to apologise for my clumsiness, but just then other men got involved and curses and fists began to fly. I cannot explain how it all happened. I don't even know exactly *what* happened; but the colonel, the large labourer, Rafferty, the Reverend, myself, and even Mycroft ended up in some confused melee of kicking feet and flying fists.

When it was all over, the colonel lay upon the floor, apparently stunned. I immediately ran over to offer him medical attention, one military man to another. Mycroft quickly called over the men from Scotland Yard. I was shocked by that; certainly as gentlemen we could work out this little mix-up among ourselves without bringing in the police?

I helped the colonel to his feet, but just then the large labourer and that Rafferty lout firmly pushed me aside, away from the poor man I was trying to help. 'What is the meaning of this?' I barked in rage that a fellow military man should be treated so shabbily, and in my own home.

'We'll take it from here, Watson,' I heard the voice of Sherlock Holmes speak up suddenly, though I did not see him anywhere. I looked quickly into the faces of the men around me but did not see him.

Mycroft just smiled.

The Reverend James glared at me.

Then I saw the colonel briskly being handed over to Gregson and Lestrade by, of all people, that Rafferty fellow, who was holding up a rather wicked-looking knife that he had apparently found concealed in the colonel's uniform. Rafferty gave it to Lestrade, saying, ''ere you go — the knife he planned to plant in Mr. 'Olmes' 'eart!'

I looked at him, aghast. What was the meaning of this? I saw now that Rafferty was aided in this action by the large oaf, the party-crashing labourer. I barely knew what to make of it all. Then I heard the voice again.

'Over here, Watson.'

'Where?' I said, and turned to look upon Rafferty. He smiled at me, showing blackened teeth; then he pointed to the large oaf beside him — the labourer. I did a double take.

'Hello, Watson,' the man said simply.

'Hello . . . Holmes? Is it truly you?' I asked in awe, watching as a miraculous transformation quickly took place before my eyes. Now the man I thought to be some heavy drunken labourer who had crashed Holmes' party for the food and rum began to shed his disguise. I watched with astonishment as he suddenly withdrew multiple wads of padding from his waist to slim down appreciably. He became rail-thin.

'Yes, good old Watson, it is I,' the man said. I watched with astonishment as he took off what was a fake nose, removed a face full of faux whiskers, and withdrew something from his mouth that had distorted his entire face, making it unrecognisable. Now I saw plainly that the man before me was, in fact, my friend Sherlock Holmes.

'How? Why?' I stammered, full of

questions. 'And the colonel?'

'Not the colonel, but Miles Abercrombie, come here to murder me,' Holmes explained. 'I put the man away years ago, and upon his escape he came here to pay me back in kind.'

I looked at my friend in awe. 'I can't believe it is you, Holmes!'

'Believe, Watson,' he said with a wry smile.

'And — that Rafferty fellow? Who the blazes is he? For a while I even thought he might be you in disguise,' I stated, now watching Lestrade and Gregson busy putting manacles upon the colonel — I mean Abercrombie. Then two stout bobbies came to escort the man out of 221B and back to prison.

'Ah, yes, Mr. Rafferty . . . ' Holmes mused thoughtfully.

'Just Rafferty, if you please, Mr. 'Olmes,' he said with a lopsided grin.

'Yes, Rafferty. Well, Watson, perhaps you remember Shinwell 'Porky' Johnson from the 'Illustrious Client' case of two years pervious? I did a bit of disguise work on his face as well, but I am sure he must have looked familiar to you.'

'Indeed he did, Holmes, but I could not place him. So Mr. Johnson was your partner in this case?' I asked, somewhat hurt by the realisation.

Sherlock Holmes laughed gently, put his hand firmly upon my shoulder, and said, 'Good old Watson. No one can ever replace you. But I could not allow you to be put in such jeopardy with Abercrombie running lose. In any event, it was hardly a case at all. Porky is a hardened street tough and a good, stout fellow in a brawl. I was sure I might have need of his skills to take down Abercrombie, before he took me down.'

'You were playing a dangerous game, Holmes.'

'Indeed, Watson. Miles Abercrombie is a deadly fellow, but your party scheme proved to be the ideal cover for what I had in mind. It all worked out quite well, allowing me to smoke him out of hiding where he could be recaptured.' Then he added, 'But I apologise for being so difficult with you about the party. Please be assured it was all done for your own protection. The less you knew about this little problem, the better for your safety — always a matter paramount in my mind, old friend.'

Holmes' words had touched my heart, and they did much to assuage my anger over his actions the recent month. Now that he had taken off all of his disguise material, he was the fellow I always recognised.

'Sorry, Watson, but when Mycroft sent me this intelligence I went to Lestrade to invite these men here. I dare say I do not like parties at all, but this one certainly went as I would have wished. By the way, I did rather enjoy your little speech, though it rang a bit too much like a eulogy for my taste. I thank you for your kind words, but I am not quite ready for retirement yet — permanent or otherwise.'

'Of course.' I smiled, then looked at my friend and asked, 'Well, now that it is done, will you at least have a glass of rum punch with me to celebrate your fiftieth year?'

Holmes' smile was broad and warm. 'Why, I would be delighted, Watson. You know, you really have done a fine job with this party.'

'Well, Mrs. Hudson helped,' I said as we clinked our glasses together. Then I said, 'Happy birthday, Sherlock.'

'Thank you, John,' he said as we downed our drinks.

There was then a brief lapse of silence between the two of us, just two old friends sharing a drink together.

Holmes smiled broadly. 'I really must commend Mrs. Hudson on her rum punch. It has quite the kick.'

'I had her make it especially for you.'

'Well, Watson, you and Mrs. Hudson have excelled with this party — in all of its aspects. I thank you sincerely.'

'It is nothing, my friend,' I replied, grasping his shoulder in stout fellowship.

'No, it is very much something, and I truly thank you for it,' Holmes spoke softly to me; then in a much firmer voice he added, 'Especially since this is the last time I will ever allow you to throw me a birthday party.'

'We shall see about that!' I replied with a laugh.

'Yes we shall,' Holmes gently chided. 'But for now, let us get a piece of that delicious-looking cake. I swear you have put Mrs. Hudson's homemaking abilities to the test this evening, but she has come through with flying colours as usual.'

'Why thank you, Mr. Holmes,' Mrs. Hudson broke in with evident delight. For once it appeared she was getting the last word as she quickly passed my friend a plate with a large piece of chocolate cake upon it. Then she gently kissed his cheek and said, 'And a very happy birthday to you, Mr. Holmes.'

HISTORICAL NOTE:
While Doyle and Watson were rather vague on the dates of Sherlock Holmes' birth, scholars over the years have pretty much all agreed upon the year of 1853 as the year of the birth of the great detective — and Sherlockian scholars often do *not* agree upon very much! So I think we can take this date to the bank. The year of 1903 would be Holmes' fiftieth year celebration, certainly a milestone that Watson would want to commemorate.

While well-wishers today sing what has become commonly known as the 'Birthday Song' at such events, the song we all know today was not even written until 1912. So any song that would be sung for Holmes' birthday celebration in 1903 would have to be something else. There would be nothing better or more appropriate than the very British drinking song, 'For He's A Jolly Good Fellow' — though I am sure Sherlock Holmes would never have thought of himself as 'a jolly good fellow'!

Sherlock Holmes –
Stymied!

'I see you have been unable to resist the allure of the links once again,' my friend Sherlock Holmes said to me one afternoon upon my visit to our old digs at 221B Baker Street. He was running his eyes over my attire with disdain, having obviously surmised that I had come over straight from playing a round of golf.

I nodded my acknowledgement. Since my marriage and the sometimes heavy workload at St. Bart's, I'd seen Holmes only sparingly during the last year, so these occasional visits were moments of great joy for me to meet with my old friend again and catch up on his cases. My only spare time of late had been taken up with my new guilty indulgence — that fascinating creation called golf.

'A most stimulating and enjoyable exercise,' I told my friend.

'Hah!' Holmes huffed sarcastically. 'A gross and unmitigated waste of time. Adult men chasing around a little ball in a game of simple and utter luck. I'm afraid *that* is not for me.'

'It is a sport, Holmes, not merely a game,' I countered, inexplicably upset by his words and feeling it was somehow my duty to defend the sport. 'I have found it an enjoyable pursuit over the last few months, and have even been invited to play at some of the most prestigious courses in England and Scotland, including the very home of the game, the Royal and Ancient Golf Club at Saint Andrews. I have even become friends with Tom Morris himself, Old Tom Morris as he is called; a legend of the game. I tell you, it is not a matter of luck; it is fraught with hazards and challenges that require a high level of skill.'

Holmes brushed all this aside with a casual wave of his hand. If it was not criminal in nature, or did not fall within the narrow scope of his interests, he was rarely engaged.

'You know, Holmes,' I told him,

allowing a hint of annoyance to enter my voice, 'we are now four years into the twentieth century — a time for new beginnings and newer things, such as golfing. The game has lately set up strict rules of play affecting every contingency. I would think this is one aspect of it that you would find appealing and even approve of.'

'Rubbish! You mentioned rules as in a sport, yet you yourself just called it a game. Checkers would be more stimulating.'

'Oh come now, Holmes!' I retorted peevishly.

'You yourself called it a game,' he countered with a wry grin.

'That was merely a figure of speech.'

Holmes looked at me, shaking his head in mock despair. 'Poor, poor Watson, I am saddened to hear that you have succumbed to the frippery of such a game of chance. Far better to spend your time and your meagre funds on the roulette wheel. Better odds, eh?'

'I beg to disagree. I have found there is great skill involved in every aspect of golfing, from the opening drive down the fairway to the chipping, and of course putting on the green. It can be most stimulating and challenging. You of all people should not be so quick to disparage a game — or dare I say sport — which you have never once tried yourself.'

Sherlock Holmes looked thoughtful, and then gave me a wry grin. 'You have me there, old fellow. You may be correct. Perhaps someday we shall have a go at it.'

'I would be most delighted to do so, Holmes. Perhaps when you are not so heavily engaged with cases?'

'Well, Watson, you have come at the perfect time. Cases have been few and far between lately. It seems the criminal classes have gone on holiday. Most disappointing.'

I laughed at his dilemma. 'Well, I am sure something of merit will turn up soon.'

'Obviously it will; but tell me more of this golfing mania you have contracted like a bad London cold. I see that there is something that evidently disturbs you about it.'

I looked at Sherlock Holmes closely. The man was remarkable. So far I had been quite careful, through neither word nor gesture, to let on to him the true nature of my visit. 'You are as perceptive as ever. How did you guess?'

'Guess! Did you say 'guess'?'

'I meant . . . What I meant to say . . . ' I fumbled quickly.

'Never mind, old boy.' Holmes smiled indulgently at my discomfort. 'Put it down to my knowledge of your person through our long association. I can see there is something bothering you, and yet you are loath to bring it up, though it pricks at you nevertheless. It is about this game of yours, is it not?'

I sighed. 'Yes, Holmes. It is a most depressing problem, but surely it does not rise to the level where your magnificent talents need to be employed.'

'Why not let me be the judge of that? As I told you, interesting cases are scant right now, so if you have something of merit I should be happy to hear the details.'

I nodded with relief that my friend was

concerned, collected my thoughts, and then began my narrative as I sat down in my old chair across from his own. 'You are correct that it has to do with golfing. I have already mentioned that I have made the acquaintance of Old Tom Morris. He is a most decent and gentlemanly fellow. These days he is the greenkeeper at the R&A, the Royal and Ancient Golf Club at Saint Andrews, in Scotland.'

'Yes, where they play the British Open. I believe Old Morris even won the championship four times in the '60s?' Holmes stated.

'Why, yes.' I smiled. 'So you know something of the game?'

'A niggling bit here and there. I heard about the fellow primarily through the mystery that befell his son, Young Tom Morris.'

'Young Tom?' I asked casually, but curious. 'I had not heard.'

'A most tragic affair, Watson. Old Tom's son, Tommy — these days known as Young Tom — was a golfing prodigy. He was a legend in his own time who followed his father into golfing history by winning four British Opens. He was young, barely twenty-four years of age, when his wife and child died in childbirth. Young Tom died three months later on Christmas Day 1875 of unknown causes. It was all quite mysterious, but most people at the time blamed it on a broken heart.'

'A sad tale,' I said softly.

'Sadder still was the loving father's reply when asked if such a death could be possible.'

'What did he say, Holmes?'

'It is said Old Tom replied that if it were possible for a person to die from a broken heart, then he would surely have died himself at the time.'

I sighed. 'That is sad. I had no idea.'

'Old Tom has outlived his son by a quarter of a century. By all accounts, he is a man of unique and outstanding character and talents. I should very much like to meet him some day,' Holmes stated. Then he looked directly at me and asked, 'So now, Watson, tell me what you came here for.'

'Well, Holmes, the Open will be

concluded tomorrow evening with the presentation of the Championship Cup to the winner — it is a large silver trophy more commonly known as the Claret Jug. The problem is, the Claret Jug has gone missing.'

'Is this jug valuable?' Holmes asked with more interest now.

'Yes — sterling silver, worth a considerable sum; but it is priceless to the club.'

Sherlock Holmes nodded, looked at me from his seat and said calmly, 'Tell me, has anyone at the club gone missing as well?'

I looked at Holmes and shrugged. 'No, not that I know of. However, Old Tom mentioned to me that one of his boys, a caddy, has been ill and not reported to work for the last two days. Old Tom says it is most unlike the lad not to be available for any match, much less a championship.'

'And is this boy interested in the game?'

'Well, I assume so; most of the caddies are enthusiastic about golfing. Old Tom told me this boy is well-mannered but rather more fanatical than most about the game.'

'I see,' Holmes said thoughtfully. Finally he looked up at me with an inexplicable smile upon his face. 'Well, Watson, you must know there is little I can do about this here in London.'

'I understand, Holmes,' I replied softly, feeling defeated, but grateful he had at least listened to my story. 'It's just that Old Tom is very upset over the loss of the trophy. It will be a disaster for the Open, for the club, and for the game of golf itself.'

Holmes suddenly stood up from his seat and looked at me sharply. 'Well then, there is nothing else to do but set off for Scotland at once and remedy this situation. Come, Watson. The game — of golf this time — is afoot!'

★   ★   ★

Due to the efficiencies of the British railway system, Holmes and I reached Saint Andrews in no less than eight hours; and once at the club, I introduced the great detective to Morris. Old Tom had also been a winner of the British Open no less than four times, but these days he was a famous ball-maker, club-maker and course designer. For many years he had been the head greenkeeper at Saint Andrews.

Old Tom Morris certainly looked every one of his 83 years of age, sporting a long, flowing white beard that rested on the center of his broad chest. He was dressed in golfing attire, a sporting jacket and plaid cap on his grey head. His left hand often rested in his trouser pocket, where he kept an ever-present pipe; and he used an upside-down hickory-shafted mashie niblick as a cane. While he never seemed to smile, his piercing blue eyes exuded intense energy and gentle kindness.

I introduced the golfing legend to the detective legend.

'Ach, as I live and breathe, can it be none other than Mr. Sherlock Holmes come hither to Scotland to visit our lovely club?' Morris asked with a thick Scottish brogue and a joyful face that lit up with mirth. He proved a most hearty and cheerful fellow. While it appeared he never cracked a smile and was the epitome of the dour Scot, Old Tom was truly a kind and warm-hearted man. His eyes fairly twinkled as he spoke. 'I am so honoured to meet you, sir, and I welcome you to Saint Andrews. I assume Doctor Watson has told you about our little problem?'

'Yes, he has. That is why I am here, Mr. Morris.'

'Well, I thank you; but please, just call me Old Tom, good sir.'

Holmes allowed a warm smile, 'Well, Old Tom, you have a missing trophy, and I hear the presentation is later this evening?'

'Aye; the championship is just finishing up and we find ourselves in dire difficulty,' Old Tom said sadly. 'The Claret Jug, as it is called, has permanently resided at the R&A since 1873. The trophy is presented to the winner of the British Open each year and gets to keep it for a year before returning it, thence to be passed on to the next champion. It had lately been returned to the club by last year's winner, but now it has gone missing. I fear it may even have been stolen.'

'The good doctor has told me that one of your boys has been ill and not turned up for work.'

'Why yes, that is true. Young Daniel Roberts — a caddy; a good boy.'

'And where may we find young Mr. Roberts?' Holmes asked.

'In the village. He lives with his mum over her dressmaker's shop.'

Holmes nodded. 'Then let us repair there immediately, for we have no time to lose.'

★   ★   ★

When we reached the home of the boy, we found young Daniel Roberts upstairs in his room in bed with an apparent dire illness of unknown origin. With the consent of his mother, and under Holmes' instructions, I quickly attended to the boy, giving him a thorough medical examination. Finally I walked outside the room to confer privately with my friend.

'Well, Doctor, what is your diagnosis?' Holmes asked me.

'There's nothing physically wrong with the boy at all. But he is terrified of something that he is desperately trying to hide. His heart is pounding fearfully from it.'

Holmes just nodded, then walked back into the room with me. There we saw Old Tom and Mrs. Roberts looking sadly upon the boy lying so sickly in the bed. The boy saw us enter and coughed lightly.

Holmes grew grimly serious. 'This will not do, Daniel. Doctor Watson has given you a thorough examination. There is nothing wrong with you. I know you are feigning illness. Time is passing. You must tell me what you did with the Saint Andrews trophy.'

The boy's face fell into despair. He was trapped, and looked over to his mother.

'Daniel Roberts, now you tell these men the truth!' the boy's mother commanded.

Daniel looked shocked, fearful with

despair, but he did not reply.

'I know you stole the trophy, young man,' Holmes declared. 'The game is up, so you may as well make a clean breast of it now.'

'Come on, lad, 'tis time to speak up,' Old Tom prompted, looking dour and disappointed that one of his boys had actually stolen the famed trophy.

The boy began to cry.

'Come now, Danny,' Old Tom added gently, 'tell me what happened. Why did you steal the trophy? Who did you sell it to?'

'Oh no, that's not the way it was at all, Mr. Tom,' the boy blurted through tears. 'I took it when the previous winner returned it to the club a few days ago. I just wanted to see me name on that trophy like all the great golfers of years before, because one day my name could be etched there too. So I used some ink to write me name there, right below Young Mr. Tom's last win from '72, I did.'

'Danny Roberts, you didn't!' his mother shouted angrily.

Holmes motioned her to silence. 'Go

on, Danny. Where is the trophy now? Did you sell it?'

'Sell it? Of course not, sir! I would never think of such a thing,' the boy stammered, obviously upset at the very thought.

'Then what did you do with it?' Old Tom prompted.

Danny looked grim, his wide eyes pleading with Old Tom. 'I'm so sorry. I was scared, sir. I know I did wrong by putting me name there, and was trying to remove it, but it just would not come off. I was terrified! Then I got the idea to take the trophy down to the stream to use the water to wash off the ink. To my relief my name came off, but then I dropped the trophy in the stream. It went in deep.'

'So why didn't you dive in after it?' I asked the boy.

Danny looked up sheepishly. 'I can't swim.'

'I see,' Holmes said, hiding a wry grin.

Danny went on to explain, 'I was fearful of disappointing Mr. Tom. He's been so good to me and all. He always told me how golf teaches responsibility and good sportsmanship — then I failed him. So I pretended to be ill so I would not have to face him. I am sorry, Mr. Tom.'

Old Tom smiled gently. 'Think no more of it, lad.'

'Will I be going off to prison?' the boy asked nervously.

Old Tom laughed with gentle warmth. 'Of course not, Danny.'

'So where's the trophy now?' Holmes asked.

'Why, still at the bottom of the stream, where I left it,' Danny replied.

Holmes nodded. 'Very well, then. Now, Danny, get yourself out of that bed and let us go and fetch it immediately.'

★　★　★

It was early the next morning when Sherlock Holmes and I played our first round of golf. The problem of the day before had been solved satisfactorily; the trophy had been retrieved and then presented in time to the championship winner with nary a hitch. Young Danny had been suitably chastised by Old Tom, but was allowed to keep his position as a caddy at the club. Once again all was right and well at the R&A.

That next day offered us a lovely brisk Scottish morning, perfect for a round of golf at the Royal and Ancient Saint Andrews. Old Tom had made a gift of a favourable tee time to Holmes and myself in gratitude for our deed, so my companion reluctantly agreed to play a round. We decided to play a singles match, just he and I, stroke play. Old Tom and Danny even volunteered to act as our caddies, each giving us much-needed and helpful instruction and information before we began play.

The course at the R&A was sandy in nature, with small hills that played havoc with even the most well-struck drive, frequently knocking the ball devilishly off-line and into an insidiously placed pot bunker that only the most diabolically warped mind could have created. It was a challenging course to play.

The first hole, known as the 'Burn' hole, was a par four. With a good deal of luck, Holmes and I both bogied it with five. We were lucky to shoot only one stroke over par. I did better on the second hole, actually making par, while Holmes did better than me on the third. By the fourth hole I began to realise that Holmes seemed to know a lot more about playing golf than he'd ever let on to me. We played a few more holes and we did well enough, mostly through the good advice of our caddies, both of us going over par of course, but not terribly so.

'Where did you learn to play so well?' I finally asked Holmes, astounded by his quality of play. I was no master of the game, nor was he, but I was surprised by the rapidity with which he had picked up the essentials.

Holmes only smiled, adjusted his deerstalker cap, and replied, 'On the train to Saint Andrews, of course. While you slept the hours away, I studied up on the game reading the golfing books in your pack. I found Horace E. Hutchinson's volume most useful, while *The Art of Golf* by Simpson was also highly informative. Did you know it even includes photographic plates of our friend Old Tom demonstrating the value of the swing? His advice is priceless. You may be correct in stating that once you understand this game, it opens up a true appreciation of it.'

'Pish, Holmes! Golf from books!' I snorted derisively, but I could not help but laud his improved attitude. 'Okay then, we'll see where this leads. We're off to the tenth. So far we are even, so let's see what you can do on the back nine.'

We moved on to the tenth hole and played through. I went ahead by a stroke, but by the next hole Holmes had drawn even with me. He went ahead on the thirteenth, but I caught up to him by the fifteenth. At this point it was anyone's game. Holmes played with grim determination, scowling at bad shots but seemingly elated when he made a good one — in that way he proved no different from any other golfer.

It was on the approach to the last hole that Old Tom announced, 'Gentlemen, the eighteenth hole. It is a par four, at 360 yards in length, and you both be even up to this point.'

'A close contest, Watson,' Holmes said ruefully. 'You are quite right, this pursuit can be most challenging. I think I shall win this hole and then put to bed once and for all your obsessive dreams concerning this game.'

'I shall give you a good fight, Holmes,' I warned.

Sherlock Holmes smiled. 'I would expect nothing less, old man.'

It had taken us each two strokes to get onto the green of the eighteenth. Holmes had a difficult 20-foot putt to make the hole. My putt was shorter, being almost 12 feet in distance. Being furthest from the hole, Holmes played first.

Holmes' putt went straight and true, right towards the hole. It looked like it just might go in. My face grew grim with the bitter taste of impending doom. Surely his ball was heading straight for the hole and would fall in right away. I looked over at my friend and he appeared elated. Then I saw his ball suddenly stop dead, less than a foot from the cup.

Holmes stared at the ball in utter shock and disbelief, as if willing it to move on its own accord and go into the cup. But it did not.

Now it was my turn. A grim smile came to my face as I prepared for my putt. Danny, acting as my caddy, took out one of his favourite hickory-shafted putting cleeks and handed it to me. 'Here, Doctor, try this one. You have a level shot; play it straight and it should go true.'

I nodded, my face serious with the competitive spirit as I got into position and made my putt. It was a less forceful stroke than my opponent's. I intended a simple and straight stroke, but my ball immediately veered off, curving in a wide arc. I shook my head with dark trepidation and took a deep breath. I saw that Holmes held his breath also.

All four of us watched intently as my ball rolled in a wide arc, slowly moving closer and closer to the cup with what appeared to be the sureness of inevitability. I let out a tense breath. It looked like I just might make the hole. Then the ball suddenly encountered a rough patch on the green, and by some devilish action hooked in front of Holmes' ball and rolled to a dead stop. I tried to figure out what had just happened. My ball now lay between Holmes' ball and the cup by barely over six inches — effectively blocking him from the cup.

'That's the way, doctor!' Danny shouted with glee.

Old Tom Morris just laughed with uproarious mirth. 'Aye, well played, Doctor Watson. It appears you've stymied Mr. Holmes quite nicely!'

'Stymied?' Holmes blurted. He was obviously not aware of this particular rule.

I was surprised myself by the turn of events, but quickly realised it could be a potential game-changer for me.

Old Tom explained, 'Watson's ball blocks your own from the cup, Mr. Holmes. It's an old and valued rule of golf called the stymie. In golf you must hit your ball true to the hole. Hence, when another ball blocks your own, you are stymied. It's your play, Mr. Holmes.'

'How can it be played if Watson's ball blocks mine?' Holmes asked.

'Indeed,' Old Tom said most sympathetically, 'the balls be just over six inches apart — so Watson's ball canna' be lifted as per the rules. Your only option is to concede the hole, or negotiate the stymie. When a player be stymied he obviously cannot putt straight for the hole, but if he strikes his ball so as to miss his opponent's ball and yet go into the hole, he is said to negotiate the stymie. Well, Mr. Holmes?'

The great detective carefully regarded his options. They were woefully limited. 'You have placed me in quite the pickle, Watson. I shall not concede the hole to you, so you leave me no alternative but to attempt, as Old Tom says, to negotiate this . . . stymie.'

'Bravo, Mr. Holmes!' Old Tom enthused warmly at my friend's obvious pluck. 'Here now, use this Jigger; it will give you the loft you need to play your ball.'

Holmes took the hickory-shafted Jigger and prepared to make his play. He took his time and hit the ball with a sudden and sharp lifting motion that lofted his ball into the air. I was shocked to see his ball ride over my own — a bare two inches in height and straight towards the hole. Then his ball kicked right *into* the hole — *and bounced right back out!* Holmes' ball slowly rolled away to rest a few inches from the cup.

It was heartbreaking. Danny grimaced, while Old Tom shook his head good-naturedly at the mystical vagaries of the game. I stood there amazed by what I had just seen. Holmes for his part said not one word; his face had become a solid mask of stone. I decided it was not the right time for me to make any comment about what had happened.

It was my turn now. I took my time. With the utmost care I took my putt, lightly tapping my ball so it fell squarely into the cup with a soft plop. I sighed with relief and looked over at my friend.

Sherlock Holmes seemed to hardly believe what had happened. A moment later he mechanically tapped his ball into the hole, officially ending the game, and then he walked away in a rather sullen funk.

I had beat Holmes by one stroke, but my victory was bittersweet. I thought I could hear my friend murmuring to himself as he walked off the green, something about how he had been right all along, that golf was a stupid game, a horrendous waste of time, and based solely upon luck rather than any true skill.

'You know, Watson, some day that damnable stymie rule will have to go,' he commented to me sharply as the four of us walked off towards the clubhouse.

Old Tom Morris cut in before I could reply: 'Never, Mr. Holmes! Not while I live! Aye, golfing tradition it surely be. One of the most sacred rules of the game.'

'Hah!' Holmes snorted derisively, dismissing the entire affair. Then he looked at me and suddenly smiled with renewed good humour. 'Well played, Watson. I must say, well played, indeed.'

'Why thank you, Holmes; that is very gracious of you. It was a close contest. I am sure you will do better on our next outing,' I said in an upbeat tone, trying to offer him some measure of support; but I knew the truth. I knew my friend. This was the first and *last* game of golf I or anyone else would ever play with Sherlock Holmes.

I shook my head in consternation as Holmes and I accompanied Old Tom towards his club-making shop off the eighteenth green. We had sent young Danny off, and now the three of us sat down enjoying a few pints, sharing stories about golf and life — and never once did we ever mention the stymie again.

HISTORICAL NOTE:

Much of the background of this story is based on historical facts that deal with the Royal and Ancient Golf Club at Saint Andrews, in Scotland; the British Open trophy, better known as the Claret Jug; and the lives of Young Tom and Old Tom Morris. I also want to thank the real Dan Roberts, as well as the Gerritsen Beach Golf Museum Library, for their assistance. In my research for this story, the exact play on the green on the eighteenth hole was set up and I was able to negotiate just such a stymie, not once but twice — so it can be done! The stymie rule was finally taken out of golf in 1952. Before then, players could not lift their ball; but after 1952 they would use a marker on the green and then lift their ball so as not to obstruct an opponent's. There are many who wish the stymie was still in effect.

The Problem at the *Musée du Louvre*

'I say, Holmes, you have a letter here addressed to you all the way from Paris!' I told my detective friend one morning as we sat comfortably in our Baker Street digs in the early autumn of 1911. The weather was brisk and the sun bright. I was considering a round of golf when I held up the unopened letter to Holmes.

'Oh, that. Be so kind as to open and read it to me, Watson.'

I carefully opened the strange foreign-looking envelope. The contents were just one sheet of paper and two tickets for the boat-train. It all seemed very mysterious. 'It is from a Monsieur Diamonde, Prefect of Police.'

'Ah, yes, Marcel of the *Surate* — a good man, Watson. He taught me the art of *savate* years ago. What does he have to say?'

'Not much, I'm afraid; just that he is in desperate need of your services upon a matter of the utmost discretion.'

'Nothing more?' Holmes asked, alert now. The letter certainly had his attention.

'No, there is nothing else written here as far as I can see,' I replied, looking it over carefully and finding nothing more there at all. I handed the letter and envelope to Holmes, who examined them in minute detail. He nodded after a long moment and then looked at me meaningfully.

'Well, then we cannot deny my old friend,' he said, stirring himself from his seat with renewed vigour. 'I smell a most interesting case. Come quickly, Watson — we are off to Paris!'

'Paris?' I blurted. 'Just like that?'

'Yes, my friend, just like that. Unless you would rather stay behind and remain here in London.'

'You know I would not!' I stated adamantly.

Holmes nodded his approval, and I wondered what it could be that might rouse my detective friend from the comfortable environs of 221B and busy London to suddenly trot off to Paris at the drop of a hat — solely upon the basis of some enigmatic note from a Parisian policeman. However, I knew that something was certainly in the works, for Holmes had traveled from England on more than one occasion on important cases when it was warranted. There was the case I had written up as 'The Adventure of the Empty House', of course — the final clean-up of the vile Moriarty gang. Moran's comeuppance had been rewarding but dangerous business. There had also been an earlier trip to France in the case of 'The Disappearance of Lady Frances Carfax', as well as travels to other countries — Switzerland in 'The Final Problem' being of most serious note. So Holmes was wont to travel if the destination promised something extraordinary upon his arrival.

I quickly collected my travel kit, packed some clothing, and made myself ready for whatever awaited us in Paris. I noticed that Holmes had thrown together some items in an old battered valise, and in short order we were ready to leave Baker Street and London.

'You have the tickets to the boat-train, Watson?'

'Of course, Holmes; they are right here.' I patted my jacket breast pocket reassuringly.

'Good!' He spoke the word in his usual excited tone when beginning what might become a promising case. 'Then we are off to Paris!'

* * *

Once in Paris, Holmes and I immediately headed to the right bank of the Seine in the first arrondissement, a most lovely neighbourhood. Prefect of Police Marcel Diamonde met us not at his office but at a venerable building or palace known as the *Musée du Louvre*, more commonly known as The Louvre.

'Sherlock Holmes, *mon dieu*! It is good to see you again after so many years, old friend!' Prefect Diamonde enthused as he firmly took my friend's hand in friendship; but instead of shaking it as in the English manner, he pulled Holmes close to him in the French fashion and then suddenly placed a kiss upon each of Holmes' cheeks. '*Mon ami*, you have not changed at all!'

I stifled a laugh, knowing all too well my friend's aversion to such overt signs of affection, even by the overly affectionate French. Nevertheless, it was plain that Diamonde was most happy to see my friend, and I could tell that Holmes was keen to see the Frenchman as well.

'Too many years have passed,' Diamonde lamented softly.

'It has been a long time, Marcel,' Holmes acknowledged with a slight nod of his head.

'And you must be Doctor Watson? It is good to finally meet you in person. I have enjoyed your recounting of Sherlock's cases in *The Strand*.'

I flushed at the praise, and we shook hands.

'And this worthy fellow is Monsieur Pierre Lamont, curator of the *Musée du*

Louvre,' Diamonde said, now introducing the man who stood quietly at his side. Mercifully, Lamont shook hands with Holmes and myself, being much more circumspect than the policeman in his greeting.

'And what can Doctor Watson and I do for you?' Holmes asked with interest as we walked the halls of the famed museum. Both Frenchmen now became suddenly mum and circumspect as to the reason they had called Holmes and myself here to Paris. It was obvious this was difficult or unpleasant for both of them to discuss.

As I walked the halls of the great building with Sherlock Holmes and the two Frenchmen, Lamont gave us a brief tour and history of the famed museum.

'We are very proud of our little museum, gentlemen. We have nearly 35,000 objects on display here, some originating from as far back as the sixth millennium B.C.,' Lamont said proudly, steering us down a large spacious hall full of priceless objects. 'The main building began as a fortress built in the twelfth century, and the actual museum opened on August the tenth, 1793 with an exhibition of 537 paintings. The museum itself today comprises an area of more than 60,000 square metres. Since then, it is of our collection of over 6,000 magnificent paintings that we are most proud . . . '

'Pierre?' Police Prefect Diamonde asked softly.

Lamont did not reply; something was obviously troubling the curator greatly. He sighed, but did not say another word other than, 'Come. My office is down this hallway.'

Holmes and I followed the curator and the prefect of police. I was taken aback by the sheer glory of so many wondrous paintings hanging on the walls all around us, as well as other artwork on display throughout the various rooms we walked through. Magnificent pieces, priceless *objets d'art*, surrounded us as we trod those hallowed halls, the sacred nature of which commanded our respect and attention.

We passed so many paintings it was

overwhelming at times, but I especially remember those by the great Jacques-Louis David, a personal favourite of mine who became the leader of the Neoclassical Movement. I was thrilled to view David's inspiring masterpiece depicting Napoleon's coronation as Emperor of France, as well as his Roman epic *The Oath of The Horatii*.

Holmes and I stopped for a brief moment to take in the terror-laden image depicted in Theodore Gericault's *The Raft of The Medusa*, a masterful recreation of the aftermath of an actual shipwreck that descended into cannibalism decades before that had shocked France and the entire civilised world. The painting reminded me of a Holmes case that was somewhat similar, which I had chronicled some years ago as 'The Loss of the British Barque *Sophy Anderson*'.

Prefect Diamonde remained silent, keeping his own counsel, while Lamont nervously looked from Holmes to myself, furtively, cautiously. 'I think it best, Monsieur Holmes, that we speak of this in the privacy of my office, do you not?'

'Of course, Monsieur Lamont,' Holmes allowed.

Once in Lamont's office, we were offered seats and tea as the furtive little curator watched us carefully, growing ever more nervous, unsure of how to begin his story.

'I have often found,' Holmes prompted softly, 'that the best place to start a story is at the very beginning.'

'Of course, monsieur,' Lamont said with a nod, determination now showing on his pale face as he pursed his lips tightly. 'It has to do with a problem with *La Gioconda*.'

'*La Gioconda*? Whatever is that?' I asked curiously.

'I believe *La Gioconda* is also known under the more common name as the *Mona Lisa*, which was on display in the *Salon Carre* for five years from 1907 to 1911 and is now on display here in The Louvre,' Holmes said softly. 'It is the famous painting by sixteenth-century Italian Renaissance artist Leonardo da Vinci.'

I had no idea he had such knowledge of

the art world, though I should have known better as his family was related to the famous French painter Vernet. So there was art in the blood, as he was often fond of saying.

'That is correct, Monsieur Holmes,' Lamont said sadly. The lack of pride in his tone was most disturbing and cause for concern.

'Oh, *that* painting,' I muttered, mindful of the famed masterwork as well as the manner in which it had once been ridiculed. I recalled much about it now. Many were outraged in 1883 when the avant-garde art world first made fun of the da Vinci masterpiece, showing a copy of the famous painting with Mona Lisa smoking a pipe, of all things, in the 'Inceherents' show in Paris.

'So what is the problem with the *Mona Lisa*?' Holmes countered briskly, chomping at the bit to get to the nub of the problem and growing impatient at the curator's delay.

'The painting is now on display on a wall in The Louvre with the title *Portrait of Lisa Gheradini, Wife of Francesco del*

Giocondo. The image is known for its enigmatic facial expression,' Lamont explained.

'The smile?' I said. 'It is well known for that smile, making it one of the most fabled curiosities of the art world.'

Holmes looked at me thoughtfully. 'Watson, old man, I had no idea you were so well-versed in art. Can you tell me what is of such particular interest concerning her smile?'

Curator Lamont spoke up quickly, 'Monsieur Holmes, the smile of the *Mona Lisa* is world-renowned for its utter incomprehensibility. I believe it was critic Walter Patur, in his 1867 essay on da Vinci, who helped popularise the image.'

Holmes looked at the little Frenchman curiously.

I jumped in: 'Holmes, there seems to be some kind of secret behind her smile — perhaps some hidden meaning? But as yet, no one has been able to find out what it is.'

Holmes nodded. 'Yes — now that you mention it, I remember seeing photographs of the painting, and recall that her smile was quite intriguing. So, Mr. Lamont and Prefect Diamonde, what exactly is your problem?'

'Please follow me, Mr. Holmes; I want to show you something and obtain your reaction,' the prefect of police said.

'Of course, Marcel. Lead the way.'

Prefect Diamonde, along with the curator, led Holmes and myself down more hallways full of priceless paintings and *objets d'art*. We were astounded by the sheer beauty and history on display before our eyes. Or at least I was — my companion seemed not to notice overly much. Perhaps he had other matters upon his mind.

We were finally brought to a large room where we could see that the entire enormous south wall was empty but for a single lonely painting. The painting was the fabled *Mona Lisa*! Truly awe-inspiring. We walked over and took it in our vision in silent amazement.

'It is truly magnificent, Holmes!' I stated, not hiding my excitement that I was in the presence of greatness in the art world. 'It is everything I have ever imagined it to be. To see it here, in person, right in front of me, has to be one of the highlights of my life.'

Sherlock Holmes stood by, firmly stoical, offering his usual calm reaction to anything not associated with crime. Art was not his forte. I was at a loss to see how he could not be moved by the wondrous da Vinci masterpiece, but I knew that was Holmes' way, so I did not expect too much of him in these matters. I did notice that soon enough he was examining the painting rather closely, even going so far as to withdraw his magnifying glass in what appeared to be some study of the paint, brush strokes, and whatever else he might have felt to be of interest.

'Ah, yes, a wonderful painting,' Holmes mumbled. 'A truly wonderful forgery.'

I looked aghast at my friend. 'Forgery, you say?'

'Absolutely, Watson,' Holmes stated with a certainty that annoyed me.

'How can that be?' I asked, astounded.

'How, indeed? What do you have to say on this matter, Marcel? I am sure you are aware this is not the true da Vinci.'

The prefect of police nodded. 'Certainly a copy — but not a forgery.'

Curator Lamont spoke up then, his hesitant voice quivering with concern and stress. 'A talented recreator, known only as Mademoiselle Lucille, made this copy of the da Vinci a year ago. I thought it rather well rendered, so I kept it. I am glad that I did. Now that the true da Vinci is missing, I am using this copy as a replacement. I could not allow the theft of the *Mona Lisa* to be known; it would destroy the heart and soul of France, and of this great museum. Monsieur Holmes, I ask if you can harness your powers to find the true da Vinci and see that it is returned to us to be hung here in its proper place. Naturally, you must use the utmost discretion in this matter.'

* * *

We were now back in the curator's office, a silent and grim quartet. Prefect Diamonde quickly spoke up, as it was apparent that the curator Lamont had suddenly suffered an attack of the cold shudders. 'My friend is obviously indisposed over this matter, Monsieur Holmes, so I shall speak for him if you do not mind.'

'I can see that. So be it.'

'Yes, well, best to get it out in the open as you British are fond of saying. Simply stated, the original painting by da Vinci has been stolen. We have no idea where it may be. We have not been contacted by anyone about it. We need it to be found, quickly and quietly. We have replaced it with a convincing copy so as not to let news of the theft get out to the public. Such a scandal would be a disaster for France and for the Louvre. Of course, it is a temporary measure, for we do not know how long we can keep this theft quiet.'

'My God!' I stammered, my outrage growing as I realised the full import of what I had just heard. 'How can such a thing happen? You have guards? Locks?'

The curator nodded his head in shame.

'Easy, Watson,' Holmes told me, grasping my arm firmly. It was a message to me to back off. I quieted down, and my detective friend now turned his attention to the police prefect. 'Marcel, what exactly has happened here?'

'*Sacre bleu!* It is terrible! As far as I can determine, the painting was stolen on the evening of August the twenty-first. Louis Beroud, a painter who helps in the museum, discovered the loss the next morning. We have no idea who took the painting, or why. There has been no contact from the thief — nor request for ransom. The museum was closed for a week after the theft was discovered for our investigation. Mademoiselle Lucille's able copy of the masterpiece was hung in the hall as a temporary replacement, but I am sure the discrepancies between the two works will be discovered before too long — Lady Lucille is certainly a good artist, but after all, she is no da Vinci.'

'Who is,' I blurted, looking at the prefect. I could not believe that they had replaced the stolen painting, thereby perpetuating an art fraud upon the public; but I suppose under the circum-stances there was little else they could do.

'Be that as it may, we need you to help us find the original da Vinci, Mr. Holmes. The Louvre — and all of France — request your assistance in this matter. Please do not refuse us.'

'I cannot refuse you, Marcel, nor France,' Holmes stated firmly.

A small smile of relief came to the face of the prefect of police. My heart bounded with pride that my friend was going to offer his services in this most perplexing matter.

'Then we must work quickly, Marcel, and you must help us as well Monsieur Curator,' Holmes stated firmly. 'Tell me, who would be likely to precipitate a theft of this particular painting, and why? First off, I want to speak to this painter, Beroud, who discovered the loss.'

'What do you think, Holmes?' I asked my friend impatiently.

Sherlock Holmes shook his head. 'You know my methods, Watson. It is always dangerous to any investigation to theorise before you have all the facts. At present, we are just beginning to obtain those facts. Marcel, let me speak to this Beroud fellow right away.'

'Of course,' the prefect replied. 'I knew you would want to interview him immediately, so I had him stand by. He is in the other room. I will bring him in now.'

Diamonde then left the room.

'Good,' Holmes said softly as he quickly brought forward two chairs from the curator's desk, placing one facing the other just two feet from each other. Holmes sat in one of the chairs and awaited the arrival of the witness.

The door suddenly opened, and into the room walked the prefect with a rather short, swarthy man whose clothing was smeared and spotted with various colours of paint.

'You are Louis Beroud?' Holmes asked quietly.

'Yes, monsieur.'

'Please be seated and tell me everything concerning your discovery of the theft of the *Mona Lisa*.'

Beroud looked nervously over at the curator, his superior, who quickly nodded for him to continue. 'Very well. It was the morning of August the twenty-second of this year. I was planning to repaint the *Mona Lisa* — Mademoiselle Lucille had recreated an able copy a year or so before — and it is a common practice for aspiring artists to recreate an old master. These are not forgeries, in case you may be thinking along those lines, sir, for the artist who copies a classical painting does not sign the original artist's name to his or her work. Just to make that clear.'

'I understand,' Holmes admitted. 'Please continue.'

'Well, there is not much to say about it. I went into the room where the painting has hung for years and saw right away that it was gone. I did not think much of it at first. I immediately went to Curator Lamont, thinking that perhaps he had had the painting taken down for cleaning or repair. I never imagined that it had been stolen!'

'Do you have any idea who may have taken the painting?' Holmes asked.

'No, monsieur. It is inconceivable — impossible! Who would do such a thing? It is one of the most famous paintings in all the world. Where would a thief even sell such a priceless object? No one would buy a stolen da Vinci.'

'No one knows it has been stolen yet,' Holmes stated, looking intently into Beroud's face.

'Oh, well then, that makes it a different matter. If the theft is not known — well, there are certain unscrupulous people in the art world who might — '

'Precisely!' Holmes said sharply. 'Can you and Curator Lamont give me a list of such people who might be interested in such a priceless *objet d'art*?'

'Yes, sir,' Beroud said. 'Of course.'

The curator just nodded, then looked to the swarthy painter and said, 'Not one word of this gets out, Beroud. You understand?'

'Of course!'

'Now give me that list of names,' Holmes commanded impatiently.

The two men wrote out a list of names, conferring occasionally, then each handed his list to Holmes. My friend looked over each list carefully, made some guttural comments, sighed, then put the lists down on the table in front of him. It appeared he had little interest in them. I wondered why. Or if it was, in fact, true that he had no interest in these lists at all — why?

'Are any of the men on these lists present or former employees of the museum?' Holmes asked, now apparently taking a new tack in his inquiry.

'No,' the curator replied slowly.

Holmes wrinkled his brow. 'Are any of these men constant visitors to the museum, or do any of them show an inordinate interest in the da Vinci painting?'

Lamont and Beroud looked at each other and shrugged. Beroud nodded, acquiescing for the curator to continue answering the question. Lamont nodded and said, 'Of course many of these men are constant visitors to the museum; several of them are enamored of the da Vinci painting — *naturalamente!* — but that alone . . . '

' . . . is not enough to cause them to be ruled a suspect,' Holmes continued. 'I understand. Now tell me this — have any of these men, or any others you may know of, shown an inordinate interest in the painting, or spoken in some obsessive manner about it?'

'Some do, yes,' Lamont replied rather unconvincingly.

Holmes nodded, but he did not look enthused. 'Can you think of anyone who would want to steal the painting, or anyone who talked about stealing it? Marcel, what about your police records? Have any of your fine French thieves ever attempted to steal, or even entertained the thought of stealing, the painting? Has there been any talk about stealing it?'

Police Prefect Marcel Diamonde shrugged. 'No, but . . . '

'But what, Marcel?' Holmes asked sharply. I looked to my detective friend and saw him wiggle his nose as if he had caught the trace of a particularly powerful odor. Something was plainly in his thoughts now.

'There are some in the bohemian crowd who often deride the painting and the museum. The poet Apollinaire is one of them.'

'Guillaume Apollinaire?' I asked, curious now, for I had heard of the fellow, even having read some of his poetry.

'You know of him, Watson?' Holmes asked me.

'Only through his work. A most able poet of the French Modern School, but one who is known for what some see as an unusual amount of anger and rage upon the subject of art.'

'Yes, Monsieur Holmes, Apollinaire once called for the Louvre to be burnt down, saying it was a repository of useless antiquarian art that has no place in the modern world, or some such disgraceful remarks; utter nonsense,' Diamonde stated simply.

'So what of this man?' Holmes asked the prefect.

'Poet Guillaume Apollinaire came under my suspicion right away, naturally, Mr. Holmes. He did once call for the Louvre to be burnt down. His words, not mine. He was arrested and placed in the Bastille. Apollinaire denied all charges, and a search of his rooms did not show anything to connect him with the theft. He did try to implicate a friend, however; another ne'er-do-well painter by the name of Pablo Picasso, who was also picked up by my gendarmes and brought in for questioning. However, both men were quickly exonerated and released. That is where the case stands now, Monsieur Holmes; and why I, with Curator Lamont, have been forced to call you in to help.'

'You did as well as possible under the circumstances, Marcel,' Holmes stated.

'What do we do now, Holmes?' I asked my friend.

'We begin at the beginning, Watson. There is something here not quite right, and we shall find it.'

'Beroud?' I asked, allowing my suspicions to show about the painter who had discovered the theft.

Sherlock Holmes shook his head. 'No, not him, but someone else. Someone close. Tell me, Marcel — and you also, Monsieur Lamont — how many former and current employees do you have in the museum?'

'Why, very many, former and current . . .'

'Go back five years for now,' Holmes asked.

The curator rubbed his face, thinking. 'I will have my secretary, Henri, bring in the employee records; but there are easily a hundred or more of them.'

'Very well,' Holmes stated simply. 'As I expected. Then, gentlemen, we shall have a long night. You should call for your people to bring into this office some urns of strong black coffee, sugar and tea, and an adequate evening meal. We are going to be here for quite some hours. We shall not leave this room until this conundrum is concluded to my satisfaction.'

'You see some answer to this, Holmes?' I asked.

'Perhaps. Now, Curator Lamont, I would like you to begin to run down the biographical particulars on each and every current and former employee. Tell me everything you know about them, along with any rumours about their personality, politics, finances, family — I want to hear it all, no matter how insignificant. I would like your secretary to also be present and add whatever he can to our search for information. Watson and I will listen intently. Marcel, can you stay to hear this?'

'Of course,' the police prefect replied. 'I hope we will learn something of value. So you believe the theft may be due to a current or former employee?'

'That is what we shall endeavour to find out. However, it will be up to Curator Lamont and his secretary, through their biographies of these employees, to give us the information we need that may lead us to our thief.'

Just then, Lamont's secretary, Henri Tassaud, came into the room with a large box of cards containing personal information on all museum employees.

'Monsieur Tassaud, I would like you to attend to us this evening and add any relevant information on these employees you may think significant,' Holmes asked the rail-thin young man.

Tassaud looked over to his employer for acknowledgement, and once given approval, said, 'Of course, sir, if I can help in any way.'

'Good; then let us begin. I assume the

records are kept in alphabetical order?'

'Yes sir, they are,' Tassaud said with pride.

'So let us being with the As, then. Who do we have first in line?'

Curator Lamont drew the first card, looked at it carefully and said, 'Bette Alban. She is a restorer who has been with the museum for five years. She is thirty-five years old and married with one small child. She has rooms in Montparnasse and does good work, but is somewhat difficult to get along with.'

'Why?' Holmes asked. Then he quickly explained, 'You and Monsieur Tassaud need to give us deeper detail on each of the people we discuss here tonight. I do not want their normal biographies only; I want to hear about their secret fears, hates, rumours about their lives, and any unusual actions or relationships. All of it. Criminal, of course, if any. And the more sordid the better. We are looking for an employee with a motive for the theft. There are many employees and many possible motives, so we have our work cut out for us this night.'

'Of course, Monsieur Holmes,' the curator stated. Then the man, with his secretary aiding him, did a systematic rendering of each employee's life, one by one. Sherlock Holmes and I, with prefect Diamonde beside us, listened intently, but we made no comments other than to occasionally ask a question to follow up on some statement or fact for clarification.

'Whatever are you looking for, Holmes?' I asked my detective friend as the long night hours wore on into the early morning, and the curator and Mr. Tassaud continued with the particulars of each current and former employee. Some of their information was most personal and, I fear, even embarrassing to the point of scandal should it ever get out. I was astonished by the rumours that were spoken about supposedly upright, God-fearing citizens. Holmes, however, seemed nonplussed by it all.

'Well, Holmes?' I asked him once more, impatient for answers.

'I have formed what I call a 'type' or 'profile' of the thief, Watson. He — for it is most certainly a man, unless I am very much mistaken — is most certainly a present or former employee of the museum. No one else could perform such a clean robbery — what seems thus far to be a perfect crime. It really is quite an accomplishment.'

'Accomplishment! I am outraged!' Curator Lamont blurted in rage.

Sherlock Holmes merely smiled, explaining, 'My good Monsieur Lamont, please understand that as a detective I can appreciate the accomplishment of such a crime — even as I seek to find the culprit and see to it that he spends many years in prison.'

Curator Lamont shook his head in dismay.

'I understand what Monsieur Holmes means, Pierre. So please do not take it the wrong way,' Diamonde explained in a soft voice.

'Yes, I apologise for any insult given,' Holmes stated sharply, almost remotely. Then he continued, 'Now you see, in a case such as this, it is sometimes advantageous to begin to solve it starting from the back end, looking at the crime and the evidence to see what they tell us about the man we are looking for. Then we seek out that man.'

'I understand that,' Prefect Diamonde added, 'but I do not see how you can use the evidence we have — as there is so little of it.'

'There you are in error, Marcel,' Holmes replied, looking up at his friend with bright, intense eyes. 'We know quite a bit about the theft, which tells us something about the thief as well.'

'How so, Holmes?' I asked. 'Quite honestly, I do not follow.'

'Yes, what are you looking for, Monsieur Holmes?' the prefect added.

Sherlock Holmes smiled indulgently. 'Patterns that fit a preconceived profile based upon the evidence we have from the crime. Our thief seems not to be the common-variety thief at all. He works for the museum, or once worked here. I am also sure he knows art and the art world. There is much more to him than at first appears. He has made no contact demanding payment for the return of the painting — no ransom for the da Vinci. Do you not find that odd? I certainly do. Neither has our thief, as far as we can tell, sold the painting to one of those unscrupulous men upon our lists of crooked dealers and collectors. No, it appears he stole the painting and is keeping it — at least for the present. I wonder why? It tells me something more about him. Whether our man plans to sell the painting later or keep it is beyond my ken at this present time to discover, but the fact that he has not quickly sold such a hot item — for surely word of it out on the market would get to us — tells me there is something more to this than just a mere theft. Our thief may, in fact, be acting as a broker to sell the painting to one of the many unscrupulous art dealers or collectors here in France, or through-out the Continent, or even in America. If that is true, then it may take some time to find him and the da Vinci.

'However, as I see it now, our man is holding on to the painting for some reason. I wonder why. Is it just that the painting is too hot to sell? But news of the theft has not got out yet, so that cannot be it. Is he merely some enamored aficionado of the *Mona Lisa* who wants it for his own personal satisfaction? Yes, that may well be, but I think there is something deeper here. I believe there is far more to this than first meets the eye. After all, our thief has accomplished a truly masterful art theft. With that in mind, I cannot believe that such a well-conceived crime would be done for the usual banal reasons. In fact, this man is a rather unique thief. So, in short, I am looking for a current or former museum employee with certain aspects that match my profile type of his personality.'

'I see that, but what might those aspects be, Monsieur Holmes?' Diamonde asked.

Sherlock Holmes allowed a wry grin. 'If and when they present themselves in a sufficient quantity in an individual, then I shall know.'

'Hah!' the prefect said in complaint. 'You cannot tell Watson and me what these aspects might be that you are seeking in your suspect?'

'No, not yet, my friend, as things are still rather fluid. You see, there are many aspects — red flags, you might call them — that draw my attention to many of these people. The foreigners, the Italians and Germans especially. There are even some British subjects, and Americans employed here at the Louvre. All pose certain challenges. There are very many variables to sift through, and as yet we have not hit upon any one man who seems right to me. So let us continue with the list of names. Where were we, Monsieur Curator?'

Curator Lamont nodded and took the next card from his secretary, Henri, saying, 'Next on the list, Monsieur Holmes, is Vincenzo Peruggia.'

'Not another Italian!' Diamonde said in evident exasperation. 'The museum employs very many foreigners.'

'They work well,' Curator Lamont offered.

'And cheaply!' Diamonde added with a grimace.

'So what of this man?' Holmes asked.

Lamont shrugged. 'No one special,

Monsieur Holmes. A middling worker, but acceptable. He is an Italian who always talks about his native land. I assume that is normal for foreigners. I found him a most annoying fellow.'

Henri added in a prickly tone, 'The man is insufferable, and often speaks badly of France. Why, he once told me we were just a pack of thieves.'

'Did he ever explain to you why he thought this way?' Holmes asked.

'No, he did not.'

'Then you did not get along well with him, I gather?'

'No, monsieur,' the secretary replied firmly.

'I see. Well then, let us continue and see what the next fellow on the list has to offer us, shall we not?' Holmes said, and the process was once more begun where it had been left off.

The lonely night continued on hour after hour as we went through name after name. This drudgery — for that was all it seemed to me — went on early into the next morning. The long list of employees — I now realised that at least one of them

Holmes considered to be a suspect — was gone through as with a fine-toothed comb.

* * *

Bright rays of the morning sun broke through the drapes of the curator's office the next morning.

'And that is all we have on Emile Zoltan. He is the last one, Mr. Holmes,' Curator Lamont told us.

Sherlock Holmes nodded, got up from his chair, and stretched his arms and legs. 'Thank you for a most interesting night, gentlemen.'

I kept silent, as I could not agree. There had been no bright flash of discovery from our work, at least not as far as I could tell. Holmes, however, seemed rather buoyant, so I wondered if he might be holding something back.

'Anything, Holmes?' I asked, curious, hoping to draw him out. I had to admit that I was dumbfounded by what we had gone through the entire night. I was dead tired, mind-numbed, as I realised that any one of two dozen people mentioned could have effected the theft. Any one of dozens — but I knew Sherlock Holmes was focused on only one of them. I just wondered which one! As yet, Holmes had said nothing to indicate who his suspect might be. I remained impatient for his solution.

'Well, Monsieur Holmes?' Prefect Diamonde asked, stifling an early-morning yawn.

'Interesting. I can tell you that the thief is a museum employee,' Holmes stated with certainty, 'but the motive and his actions I find perplexing, even rather amazing.'

'Well, who is it, Holmes?' I asked impatiently.

'Yes, who is the thief? Give me a name and I shall arrest him immediately!' Prefect Diamonde demanded.

'Not so fast, gentlemen. There is more to this than meets the eye,' Holmes replied softly. 'I need to think on this. I will get back to you by tomorrow evening. Believe me, gentlemen, we have some time on this case to ensure we see it through correctly.'

★ ★ ★

That night in our hotel room in central Paris, Sherlock Holmes and I ate a most delicious meal as we began to talk over the case of the missing da Vinci.

'Well, Watson, what do you make of it?' Holmes asked me suddenly. I was surprised that he wanted to know my opinion on the matter instead of telling me what he had discovered.

'I hardly know, Holmes. You have proved — or at least suspect — that it was an inside job; so I assume you have found a suspect?'

'Merely a suspect at the moment, but continue.'

'So if you do have a suspect, strangely you have not given the name to the police, or even myself. I wonder why?'

'Yes, the word 'why' asks a good question. There are still threads that need to be collected regarding this case. With that in mind, I have some important work to do tonight and shall be going out

146

soon,' Holmes told me in a surprise move. 'I will not be back until early tomorrow morning, but I will do something that will set this case on its head.'

'What is it, Holmes?' I asked naturally, but Sherlock Holmes would hear none of it. He was firm on his action, and would not speak another word to me until a half hour later as, dressed in dark clothing, he left our hotel room, saying, 'Good evening, Watson. I shall see you in the morning. Do try to get some sleep, as you will need to be at your best on the morrow.'

★   ★   ★

'So what were you up to last night?' I asked boldly of my friend first thing that morning.

'Ah yes, I had a most interesting and productive evening. Pity you were not with me,' Holmes told me.

'Well, can you at least explain it to me, please?'

Sherlock Holmes gave me one of his

little enigmatic grins and nodded his head. 'Of course. Last night I tracked down my suspect, entered his apartment, and let me just say that what I discovered entirely validated my suspicion of him.'

'I see. But who is he? And how did you decide that this particular man was the thief? There were so many possibilities. We went over so many museum employees in the curator's office last night.'

'No, not really — there was only one possibility,' Holmes explained. 'I was looking for only one particular type of fellow. You see, I have learned that discovering a suspect out of all the chaff of those involved in a crime must be done through looking at the patterns of their behaviour. Or if you prefer, as we did last night — what I like to call a conclusive 'profile' of the man we are looking for. The aspects of the character of the criminal and his crime tell us who we are looking for. What I only needed was the curator and his secretary to give us the biographies of each employee — along with their other more personal and secret information. This was key. It was in this way that I came across my suspect's patriotic fervour, and hence his political obsession — and the da Vinci painting just naturally fit in with the personality profile I had constructed for him. Once I had my man, I went out last night to verify my finding, and I am now able to report that I was proved correct in every aspect of my theory about him.'

'So then where did you go last night, Holmes?'

'I went to the thief's apartment, of course. He was quite easy to track down.'

'Do you think that was wise? You may have been in danger. You should have alerted Perfect Diamonde, and he could have assigned you some of his gendarmes. You could have been in danger, Holmes,' I said, for I worried about my detective friend when he went out on these nightly missions. He was not as young as he used to be.

'There was never any real danger, Watson. Regardless, our thief was out, his rooms were not occupied at the time, so I entered and had the run of the place. It did not take me long to discover something there that now makes all the difference in this case.'

I looked at him squarely. 'The da Vinci?'

'Correct, Watson. I found the painting. Then I decided to do a bit of constructive correction to this vexing problem.'

'You did not, Holmes!'

'Yes, I did, Watson.'

'So tell me the rest. Tell me all of it, please.'

Sherlock Holmes smiled at me thoughtfully. 'Watson, my suspect is one Vincenzo Peruggia, a Louvre employee and an Italian nationalist. This Peruggia is a cheeky fellow, bold and lucky. He stole the da Vinci painting right under everyone's noses and made a clean getaway. He entered the building during regular working hours, hiding himself in a broom closet of all places. When all was clear, he made his way to the da Vinci and cut the painting out of its frame, then he walked out of the museum with the priceless painting rolled up under his coat after the building had closed. No one saw a thing.'

'Amazing, Holmes!' I said, looking at my companion with awe and admiration. He had surely solved the crime, though I was soon to learn that he had done much more than that. 'I assume you told Prefect Diamonde that you solved the case, and that the rotter is even now spending the night in a cell in the Bastille?'

Sherlock Holmes did not reply.

'Holmes?' I prompted carefully. 'You did *not* tell this information to Prefect Diamonde?'

'No, Watson,' Holmes replied simply.

I was astonished. 'But why?'

'This Peruggia is an interesting fellow. He pulled off the perfect crime, and I had not the heart to see him go down for it.'

'How can you say that?' I blurted in utter surprise and in what I realised was some anger. 'You have let off a terrible thief!'

'Oh, not so terrible, I assure you,' Holmes stated simply.

I was bemused by his words but continued to press him on the matter. 'Well, a thief nonetheless.'

'Actually, the man is an Italian patriot

who stole the da Vinci painting because he believed that it should be returned to Italy for display. I must admit that I have some sympathy with his position. It is, after all, an Italian Renaissance treasure, not French.'

'But, Holmes! So what if the man is a patriot? He is also a criminal, and he must not profit from his crime,' I stated seriously.

'He will not. I made certain of that.'

'And how did you do that?'

'You remember the copy of the da Vinci by the talented artist known as Mademoiselle Lucille that was hung in the Louvre as a replacement for the missing original?'

'Why yes, of course.'

'Well, I liberated that painting from the Louvre.'

'You broke into the Louvre!' I gasped, my shock at his behaviour growing deeper by this admission.

'I did not break in, Watson. I merely took a walk through the halls after hours. In any case, it was not all that difficult, I assure you. While Curator Lamont has increased his security, I find it still to be most inadequate.'

'Nevertheless ... You ... ' I was stumped by his action, but finally only nodded. 'Oh, well, go on then.'

'Thank you. Well, as I have already told you, I tracked down this Peruggia, and I found the da Vinci, then I merely replaced one with the other. Now Peruggia has the Mademoiselle Lucille copy, still believing it to be the original da Vinci, while the original da Vinci is even now hanging in its rightful place back in the Louvre.'

'Holmes, you didn't!'

'I did.'

'Simply amazing — you surely showed him! Bravo!'

Sherlock Holmes smiled. 'I thought you would like this conclusion to the knotty problem of the lost da Vinci. Peruggia will not see prison — at least not here in France in the Bastille, or upon that hellhole of Devil's Island — and he still believes he has the original da Vinci, at least for now. As I told you, the man is a cheeky fellow. It even appears he may also have been motivated by a friend who planned to sell copies of the painting, which they assumed would skyrocket in value after the theft of the original was known.'

'Copies? Could this have something to do with the artist known as Mademoiselle Lucille?' I asked, taking his hint and running with it.

'Perhaps, but by now it is a moot point. Now all has been set right; and while Peruggia believes he has the original da Vinci, he does not. Case closed.'

'You've done it again, Holmes.'

★ ★ ★

After Curator Lamont was assured that the precious da Vinci was back upon the wall in the Louvre where it belonged — and that it was the true and original *Mona Lisa* — he was ecstatic. Prefect Marcel Diamonde admitted that he was a bit put off by my friend not offering up to him the name of the thief; but since the case was solved, the original painting returned, and the curator happy, the prefect of police had to admit that the final word on the matter, as the British are so fond of saying, is all's well that ends well.

In gratitude to Holmes and myself, we were given a personal and private grand tour of the treasures of the *Musée du Louvre* by Curator Lamont himself. Now recovered from his ordeal, he was most happy and proud to show us his special treasures, and he waxed poetic on each one while he escorted Holmes and myself from one priceless masterpiece painting and sculpture to another. It was truly awe-inspiring. I was beside myself with absolute joy — Holmes not so much. As ever, my friend's focus was upon crime and not upon art. I knew that he yearned to be back home in London doing his duty putting criminals behind bars — which made his actions regarding Peruggia all the more mysterious.

Holmes had confided to me the night before at our hotel that he was rather afraid he had allowed the criminal classes of London a sumptuous holiday by his absence in this trip to Paris.

'Fear not, Holmes,' I told him in a soft tone as we strolled the hallowed halls of the famed museum. 'You will be home soon enough, and I am sure there are plenty of convoluted cases calling out for your attention.'

'Yes, Watson, it will be good to be back home. I have to admit that this museum, while certainly criminally interesting, just poses too many vexing problems, even for one such as myself.'

I looked at my friend carefully. 'Whatever do you mean by that?'

'Why, Watson, haven't you noticed? Our friend Monsieur Lamont has quite a large problem on his hands. The missing da Vinci only opened the door to it.'

'And what might that be?'

'It is plain to see by any trained observer. The truth is, fully five percent of the items on exhibit in this museum are either fakes, copies or forgeries. Well done to be sure, but mere copies or forgeries.'

'My Lord! You are talking about dozens of items!' I blurted out in shock, then kept my silence. I was about to ask if Holmes was serious about what he had just told me, but I knew better than to doubt his words. This was ghastly!

'Actually, five percent would include 251 items; but since we have not yet viewed the entire holdings of the museum, there may be more,' Holmes stated rather mechanically.

'That is terrible!' I whispered, totally taken aback by this knowledge.

'Indeed, Watson. That is why I propose we cut short our tour of the museum, say our fond farewells to Curator Lamont and Marcel, and head back to good old London where we belong.'

I looked at my friend carefully, sighed, and said, 'I am with you there, Holmes.'

HISTORICAL NOTE:

La Gioconda, also known as the *Mona Lisa*, and painted by Leonardo da Vinci, was indeed stolen from the Louvre Museum in Paris on August 21, 1911 by employee and Italian patriot Vincenzo Peruggia. The thief simply entered the building, cut the painting from the frame on the wall, and then walked out with it rolled up under his coat. No one saw a thing. Peruggia believed that the painting, created by an Italian artist, deserved to be returned to Italy as a national treasure, and took it upon himself to do so. Peruggia kept the *Mona Lisa* in his apartment for two years until he was caught when he attempted to sell the painting to the directors of the Uffizi Gallery in Florence — where it was exhibited all over Italy and then returned to the Louvre in 1913. Peruggia was hailed for his patriotism in Italy, and he only served a few months in jail for his crime.

While this story, narrated by Watson, indicates that Sherlock Holmes made the switch of the original for the copy, there is no conclusive evidence that this was true other than Watson's own words upon the matter. For most of us, however, that would be quite enough. For others, the case of the missing *Mona Lisa* will forever be as mysterious as her enigmatic smile.

Challenger's *Titanic* Challenge

1. The Challenge Begins

McArdle had Malone on the ropes once again, this time sending his young reporter to visit the man he called 'the angry brute' because of their previous Maple White Land adventure. Malone had written that up in a series of articles in *The Chronicle* last year under the title *The Lost World*, and now the thought of facing that most difficult of men once again was certainly daunting. For the world was coming upon the one-year anniversary of the *Titanic* tragedy. The ship had gone down in icy north Atlantic waters, with approximately 1,500 passengers and crew lost. McArdle wanted a feature article on the reason behind the sinking of that most 'unsinkable' of great ocean liners upon its maiden voyage after hitting an iceberg the night of April 14, 1912.

Now, one year later, Malone was to visit Professor George Edward Challenger once again. His mission this time was to challenge Challenger, England's foremost scientific mind, to obtain his very particular theory upon the scientific reason behind the sinking. Malone was sure he was in for a most difficult and unusual situation, surely nothing he could have expected, and the professor would once again prove him correct. So Malone set off to see Challenger and accept what fury would come.

'I must admit that I am rather incompetent in this area,' Malone candidly told the professor upon his visit to his home at Enmore Park. He was a newspaper reporter, and a good one, but certainly no scientist.

Challenger smiled indulgently. 'Why, that is the most incisive comment you have made since I have known you, Malone. I am gratified when the incompetent admit their incompetence and acknowledge the superior intellect of a truly first-class mind.'

'Which, of course, you possess in abundance,' Malone dared reply; but it was in all seriousness, for he took care not to show the least bit of criticism, since he was well aware of the professor's volatile personality.

'Certainly, young man,' Challenger boomed in a blustery voice, pointing his huge black beard at his guest when he lifted his head as if it were a weapon. 'So what is it you want to know? Not another article for your Fleet Street rag, I pray.'

Malone swallowed hard, for he had come to Challenger precisely for that very reason, which he knew would surely cause the stunted Hercules before him to explode into anger and blind rage; rage that could end in violence. The two men had come to blows once before. Two years previously, at the beginning to their *Lost World* adventure, it had happened; but then Challenger's wife had intervened and thankfully saved Malone from her husband's lordly anger and those great hairy gorilla hands upon his throat. Challenger did not suffer fools — nor

161

anyone else, for that matter — lightly.

Malone grew nervous; his mind recalled those memories with grave concern. He knew he must seek a more nimble approach — however, the professor would not allow him that way out.

'Malone! You rascal!' the professor's voice bellowed in a throaty roar, as if reading his mind. Now the newsman grew fearful, for he well knew this was how it began with Challenger: working himself up into a frenzy of anger, then rage. The professor was well-known for having assaulted various impertinent persons in his career, and had been the subject of numerous court cases, so the newsman did not take his volatile anger lightly or frivolously.

'No, not I, Professor Challenger, I assure you, sir.'

'Then get to it, Malone! My time is valuable, you know! Genius waits for no man.'

Malone nodded, quickly explaining that his editor had tasked him to write a feature article about what Challenger saw as the scientific causes of the *Titanic* tragedy — if there were any.

Challenger seriously considered the premise for a moment, then suddenly boomed in agreement, 'I have thought upon that very subject since it first occurred, and have collected evidence that will shed new light upon the disaster. So I accept your request, Malone. When do we get to work?'

'Well, ah, Professor, that is the one caveat; for I will not be working with you this time. Not until I return. Professor Summerlee and Lord John Roxton are also not available.'

'What? Well explain yourself, young man!'

'Mr. McArdle is most insistent that I leave at once from Liverpool tomorrow to take ship to New York, where I am to interview the American president. Professor Summerlee is incommunicado doing research in some corner of darkest Africa, while Lord John is off hunting in the faraway jungles of Siam.'

'I see,' Challenger said unhappily. 'So I am to do all the work, spend all my time and energy, and then present to you my findings, information I researched so hard to complete? Then you write your article upon your return and take all the credit?'

'Absolutely not! No, it is not like that at all, sir, I assure you. But if you do not mind — '

'Hah! I most certainly do mind! You abuse me, my young friend!' Challenger growled, and Malone could see the rage brewing in the older man's beetling brows; his twisted mouth and his blustery manner growing dangerously close to the red zone.

'Of course not, sir! I would never be party to such a thing. Since Summerlee, Lord John and I will not be available, I have arranged for a new team to join you in this endeavour.'

'A new *team*? I need no 'team', Malone — I am my own *team*! I am simply asking for some competent assistance. I have my research notes all prepared upon this subject and have formulated my theory. Do you believe I have not thought upon the roots of this tragedy since the very moment I heard of it?'

'Of course, Professor,' the newsman replied demurely, but with all earnestness.

Challenger looked at Malone carefully,

showing his imperious and insufferable lordly manner, as his wondrous mind thought over the implications. 'Malone?' Challenger asked his guest in a quiet voice loaded with dangerous suspicion. 'By the by, my lad, just for curiosity's sake if nothing else, who have you engaged?'

Malone thought quickly; this would be a most delicate explanation. 'Well, Professor, they are three good men of note.'

'I am waiting, Malone!'

The young man swallowed hard and blurted, 'You know them, sir, or know *of* them, surely: Doctor John H. Watson . . . and the Holmes brothers.'

'Hah! Well, that is just impossible! This Watson is a medical man and may be of some use, but the others . . . the Holmes brothers, you say? I know of Mycroft certainly — a superior mind, without a doubt — but he will surely never leave the confines of his beloved Diogenes Club, so he is a non-starter. And that younger Holmes brother . . . ?'

'Sherlock.'

'Yes; that pompous, arrogant mountebank Sherlock Holmes!' Challenger boomed in rough rage.

The young newsman feared the man might turn violent any moment. Malone spoke quickly, pleadingly. 'They are all worthy fellows, Professor, I assure you, and each one has much to offer you in your great work. They are all onboard and agreeable, and only await your assent for them to join you here.'

Challenger grunted, then surprisingly shrugged his mighty shoulders. 'Well, I can stomach Mycroft Holmes and Doctor Watson well enough; I have heard both are intelligent and scientific men, after all. But this Sherlock Holmes fellow? Why is he interested in this project? I propose to you that the man has some ulterior motive for his involvement. In fact, I am certain of it.'

'It does not matter, sir, for he is willing, and so are the others; and all three, I am sure, will be of inestimable help to you.'

'Inestimable help? Malone, you are a clod; you arrange this fiasco just as you embark upon these shores by steamship on the morrow. You disappoint me, young man. Nevertheless, I am a most magnanimous fellow, as all can surely attest, so with reluctance I will agree to your offer. Very well, you may tell these men to come here tomorrow — then I shall see what their true game is!'

2. Holmes and Watson Are Drawn In

'Well, Holmes, I must say you look rather grim this evening. I gather you have heard from Malone?' Doctor Watson asked, noting his friend's intense demeanour.

'Malone and Mycroft,' Holmes replied sharply. 'This is a dangerous game. Of course, you know my brother has taken himself out of the picture, so you and I are on our own for this one.'

'Well, that is certainly not quite cricket of him,' Watson said, his feathers a bit ruffled. 'I mean, Malone enlists Mycroft's aid in something or other that he and you will not divulge to me; then Malone sails off across the Pond to New York. Now your brother opts out as well, and leaves us holding the bag.'

'I know nothing of Malone; but that is Mycroft, for good or ill, I am afraid.'

'Well, I don't like it, Holmes. We do not even have any idea why we are to see this Professor Challenger.'

'I have some idea, good Watson, and it may be of the utmost importance. Malone has engaged us, ostensibly to help the professor in some scientific research, something pertaining to the *Titanic* tragedy; but Mycroft has told me of a more pressing issue.'

'Ah, so now we get to the nub of the issue.'

'Indeed, Watson. You are perhaps familiar with the reputation of this Professor George Edward Challenger?'

'Yes, of course. I have heard the stories, and they abound. He is said to be a man of incredible intellect and just as incredible temper. He is a brawler.'

'More than that, he is a misanthrope; a man not born out of his century — but born out of his millennium,' Holmes added.

'It is no secret that even his colleagues hate him.'

'And with good reason, my friend. Professor Challenger, though a brilliant man, is certainly the most insufferable fellow in all of England. He beats the world for offensiveness. Nevertheless, we must find a way to deal with him.'

'Why is that, Holmes?'

'Because there will be an assassination attempt made upon his life in the next day or two, and we must prevent it at all costs.'

'But surely Mycroft's people, or Scotland Yard, can place guards at his home to forestall any such attempt?'

'Challenger would never accept such an arrangement. He is as impossible in that regard as in most other things. It is up to you and me to see this through. You are packed and ready to go? Very well; we leave tomorrow morning at first light, then catch our train at Victoria Station.'

3. The Detective and the Professor

'There it is, Watson — Challenger's house at Enmore Park. It has been a long trip, but we will be there soon, so steel yourself, for I assure you this man can be most difficult,' Holmes warned as the small trap, drawn by a single horse, slowly brought the pair to the front yard of the great man's home. Holmes paid the driver and Watson gathered their two small valises in hand, then with heavy hearts both men walked up the cobbled pathway to the front door.

Watson looked at that door with some trepidation, then shot a wary glance to his companion. 'Well, here we are, Holmes.'

Holmes nodded, telling the doctor, 'Go on then, ring the bell and let us begin what I am sure will prove to be a most singular adventure.'

Watson took a deep breath and rang the bell. Immediately the two men heard a loud bellowing voice roaring in answer from the other end of the house: 'Go away!'

Watson looked askance at Holmes, but his companion only smiled. 'Ring it again, old fellow.' He did as Holmes instructed.

'I told you to go away! Do not make me come out there and thrash you, for I surely will! Newsmen, drummers, inter-fering annoyances — I'll not have you! Now be gone!'

'Holmes, he sounds like a madman.'

'I have often had the occasion to notice, my good Watson, that there is a thin line between genius and madness; and I am sure Professor Challenger possesses both qualities in ample mea-sure.'

Watson shook his head in despair. Holmes himself now rang the bell, and continued to ring it again and again until they heard loud footsteps rushing upon the wooden floor inside the house advancing towards them. Suddenly the front door was flung open, and there in the doorway stood an enraged Professor Challenger: short, squat, a muscular bull with jet-black hair and a beard that jutted out at them like a dagger. His eyes were a piercing grey, his manner was arrogant and threatening, and his gorilla-like hands were balled up into massive fists that appeared ready to strike out at any moment.

In a bellowing Scottish accent he

growled, 'My lovely, patient Jessie tells me I must restrain me baser impulses to pummel those who would disturb me from my work.'

Watson looked upon the man in utter amazement, wondering if he should have brought his revolver.

Holmes allowed a wry grin, and simply offered his hand in greeting, 'I am Sherlock Holmes, and this is my friend and colleague Doctor John Watson. Have I the pleasure of addressing Professor George Edward Challenger?'

'You know you do, sonny!' Challenger blurted; then he reluctantly nodded, but he did not shake hands with Holmes. 'All right then, come in. I told Malone I would see you, and I always keep my promises; but for the love of God I cannot see what either of you men could contribute to my research upon the *Titanic* disaster. In fact, I am almost complete with that work, so I have no need of your help. As if you could offer any!'

'Really?' Holmes asked, carefully diplomatic, knowing full well that he needed to tread lightly with this man as he entered his house. 'I am happy to hear that news, and would be most eager to view your findings.'

'If you could understand them,' Challenger growled, looking at the great detective carefully. 'The world is full of obtuse clods I am forced to contend with!'

Holmes smiled calmly. 'I see.'

Watson had heard enough by then. He stammered in anger, 'Well, really, Professor! I am astounded! You present to us a most rude and offensive manner!'

'Easy, my friend,' Holmes cautioned the doctor; but it was too late, for Watson was now on fire.

'No, Holmes, I'll not stand by and listen to this bombastic bore speak to you in such an arrogant manner! He is abominable! We come here to help him, and this is the treatment we receive! I'll not countenance such behaviour from this bearded popinjay!'

'Popinjay!' Challenger barked in rage. 'I'll show you what a popinjay can do!' Suddenly Challenger crouched down into a low attack stance and charged Watson head-on like a wild bull.

Watson was utterly surprised and totally taken aback by the sudden and most ungentlemanly attack, but Sherlock Holmes had expected just such a situation. He deftly lifted an umbrella from the nearby stand and, upending it, used the hook to grasp the Professor's leg to quickly bring him down to the floor before he could reach Watson.

Challenger hit the floor, bellowing in anger, fuming, and roaring in rage. 'I was tricked! That was entirely unfair of you, sir!'

'And I suppose I should have allowed you to pummel poor Watson here,' Holmes stated firmly with cold precision and total control. 'I think not. He and I are here at your invitation. I am most disappointed in you, Professor, most disappointed. You are one of the most brilliant men in the British Isles, even in the entire world. It is a shame you resort to such barbarous tactics and cannot control your anger. It is, I must say, quite disgusting. Come, Watson, let us leave this man and his house immediately.'

'George! George, what have you done?' This now from a high-pitched female voice belonging to a slim, petite, bird-like woman who had just run into the room. It was Challenger's wife, Jessie, and she rushed to her fallen husband.

'Are you all right, dear?' Jessie asked the much-chastened professor as she helped her husband to his feet, for Holmes' words had had a most intense effect upon him.

'Yes, my love,' Challenger said softly, giving his wife a soft kiss upon the cheek. 'I am fine, fine I tell you. Now you should get back to your sewing and have no further worries on my behalf. This is Doctor Watson and Mr. Sherlock Holmes. Malone enlisted them to help me, and — '

'And you lost your temper again, George, did you not?' his wife scolded him firmly.

'Yes, I am afraid I did, my love.'

'Then an apology is in order, is it not, George?'

'Yes, of course. I am sorry, my dear,' Challenger said softly.

'Not to me, you ninny, but to these two gentlemen,' Jessie instructed him.

Challenger smiled broadly at the rebuke. 'Just teasing you, my dear. Yes, of course. Please accept my apology, gentlemen. My words were abominable, but I find these days that I am inundated with too many people, all of whom intrude upon my time and my work. Both of which are precious to me.'

'As they should be,' Holmes stated, his eyes upon those of the professor. 'Let us speak no more of it.' The great detective held out his hand once again, and this time Challenger took it and shook it heartily. Then the same was done with Watson.

'Good, now I will leave you gentlemen to your important work,' Jessie Challenger told them as she left the room.

Challenger smiled a broad grin through his thatch of great black beard as he watched her walk out of the room. 'That little lady is the love of my life, sirs. I have no idea how she can still put up with me after all these years, but she does.'

'You are a most lucky man,' Watson stated sincerely.

'You are correct, Doctor,' Challenger said as he led his two visitors into his large and comfortable study, closing the door behind him and then offering them seats. 'Now tell me the real reason why you are here, Mr. Holmes.'

'To aid you with your research,' Holmes replied simply. 'Malone said you needed some helpers.'

'Hah! That's a crock! I need no helpers — and in any event, my research is all but completed. I have come up with a fascinating theory, something so earth-shaking that it may be decades — or even a century — before the world will be ready to understand it.'

'Indeed,' Holmes said, very much interested. 'I would be delighted to hear about it. I am sure anything you have discovered will set conventional scientific thought upon its head.'

Challenger preened a bit at the compliment. 'It certainly will, Mr. Holmes; but at this moment I want the truth of your visit here. The real reason.'

Holmes nodded. 'Very well, Professor. Within the next forty-eight hours, an assassination attempt will be made upon your life.'

Challenger was silent for a moment with this grim news; then he laughed uproariously. 'Bah! Nonsense! I receive death threats all the time. Why, I am sure that half of my colleagues would murder me in my very bed if they had the nerve to do so and could guarantee they would get away with the crime. You have to do better than that. I do not believe you.'

'Believe what you will, Professor,' Holmes stated firmly, 'but Watson and I are here to forestall that attempt. I cannot tell you from what source it will come or who is directly behind it, but I can tell you it is not a crime born out of passion of any type. It is a professional job.'

'Professional, you say?' Challenger asked, thinking it over. It certainly sounded ominous.

'Absolutely. Professor, I know that a brilliant man such as yourself works upon many research projects simultaneously. One of these may have attracted the attention of a foreign power. Watson and I are here to prevent the murder of the world's greatest scientist — a man who possesses a brilliant mind of the very first order, which cannot be allowed to be shut down. It would be a tragic loss to the Empire — to humanity itself!'

'Yes, surely it would,' Challenger stated in all seriousness. 'But how do you know this? Ah, yes, of course — your brother, Mycroft. So what is the plan?'

'Someone will show himself here within the next forty-eight hours. Until that time, Watson and I will be honoured to be your guests and endeavour to help with your *Titanic* project in any way we are able.'

Challenger nodded, accepting the terms; then a worried look came to his face. 'Tell me, Mr. Holmes — is this assassination connected in any way to my research upon the sinking of the *Titanic*?'

Holmes allowed a slim grin. 'Most assuredly not.'

'I presumed so. Nevertheless, I am gratified to hear it. It would grieve me severely if that great tragedy and loss of life were the result of anything other than cruel fate — as in some man-made incident.'

'I assure you it was not,' Holmes confirmed.

Challenger nodded in relief. 'Well, gentlemen, Malone organized this meeting but I fail to see how you can aid me in my scientific research. All it needs now is for Malone to return later this month and write up my findings for publication.'

'Then perhaps Watson and I could be of some little help. As men of natural inquisitiveness, we have our own theory about this tragedy, but would be most pleased to hear yours. Eh, Watson?'

'Absolutely, Holmes,' Watson replied, looking towards the black-haired bull-like man seated behind his desk. 'Professor Challenger, I cannot begin to tell you how thrilled I am to make your acquaintance — I have followed your exploits in the scientific journals, and your work is unparalleled.'

'Naturally,' Challenger asserted boldly, enjoying the prestige the doctor had bestowed upon him. 'Then I shall explain to you my findings, so long as you both are capable of understanding them.'

Holmes shot Watson a sharp look of restraint, and the two men patiently waited for Challenger to begin his explanation of the great steamship tragedy.

Challenger began in his great booming voice: 'Science, sirs, is a living, breathing, turbulent game. The minute one new discovery has been made, it becomes obsolete as the world breathlessly awaits for the next one to be made. I feel I have jumped ahead — perhaps by decades — in my findings. I have prepared voluminous books of calculations proving my findings beyond any doubt. I will allow you and the doctor to read them first-hand tomorrow morning. As for now, good sirs, it is rather late, and Jessie calls us to dinner.'

The two guests then dined with Challenger and his delightful wife. Both men were rather astounded by this pairing of the larger-than-life misanthropic little Hercules with such a petite and bird-like woman. But the love was certainly there for the guests to plainly see. For Jessie doted on her husband as though he were a young precocious boy of twelve years; and for all his terrible ways, Challenger's gruff edges softened to putty at her loving manner.

The foursome enjoyed a fine meal; and afterwards, Challenger — knowing something of Mr. Holmes' reputation from Doctor Watson's stories in *The Strand* — called upon his guests to recount one of their most famous cases.

The evening concluded with Challenger giving vent to his own opinions on every topic under the sun. Like an angry lord or some Olympian god of old, he railed against the impurity of science and the clods who were his colleagues. Finally it was time for bed, and Jessie led Holmes and Watson to an upstairs spare bedroom, for the professor would not hear of his guests seeking a hostelry in the local village for the night.

Once Holmes and Watson were alone, the two men were able to speak freely out of the range of Challenger's hearing.

'I am much relieved the professor

invited us to stay here tonight, Watson.'

'Yes, these accommodations are far superior to those any local village inn could provide,' Watson replied, unpacking his small valise.

Holmes smiled indulgently at his friend. 'That is not the reason I had in mind. Challenger is in danger, so it is good we are here in his home to stand watch. With that said, I will take the first four hours and you the second four, old fellow. Is that acceptable?'

'Whatever you say, Holmes.'

'Good man. Now get some sleep. I will wake you in four hours.'

Watson went to bed and was soon asleep, snoring rhythmically as Sherlock Holmes stood alert guard, in deep thought on what the morrow would bring.

4. Challenger's Challenge

The night passed without incident, and Holmes was sure that was only because of Watson's and his own presence in the house. After dressing, the two guests joined Challenger and his wife in a delightful morning meal before getting to work.

'I am something of an amateur astronomer, gentlemen, and enjoy keeping records of the events of the heavens that I observe with my telescope. I keep voluminous notes,' Challenger explained, leading Holmes and Watson to his study. There he picked up two heavy foot-thick binders into his large hairy hands. Carrying one massive binder under each arm, he then led his guests outside the house to chairs upon the patio, surrounded by a lovely garden and lush bushes.

'My Jessie suggested we get out of my stuffy study and enjoy the morning air out here in the garden; and of course, she is correct. So sit down, gentlemen, and relax,' Challenger said as he seated himself in a chair across from his guests and presented Holmes and Watson each with one of the massive binders.

'What is this?' Watson asked in some wonderment.

'My work, Doctor; the facts and figures of it all. Read it, and it will make all as clear to you as the morning sun,' Challenger ordered in a blustery roar.

'Why, it must weigh ten pounds!' Watson said in astonishment, taking the massive tome and looking at it with grave misgiving.

'Only a little over eight pounds, I assure you. I despise padding in scientific calculations. But it is all there, not one wit more or one wit less,' Challenger stated proudly.

'And what are we to do with this, Professor?' Holmes asked calmly.

'Do? Why read it, of course, sir! Read it and learn the brilliance of my discovery!'

Holmes allowed a grimace as he leafed through the massive compilation. Challenger noted the gesture and grew a bit piqued, but Holmes quickly worked to tamp down the man's rising mood. 'Professor, there is no doubt your brilliant discovery here is an important one, and will offer new information on the *Titanic* tragedy; but poor Watson and I are not scientists, and certainly we do not possess minds that are in your intellectual league.'

'That is true, of course,' Challenger allowed, staring suspiciously at the two men, 'but you should not deride yourselves for your lack of intellect.'

Holmes nodded, allowing a tiny smile.

Watson looked imploringly at his detective friend, then to Challenger. 'You expect us to read all this? Now, at this moment? Why, it must run to a thousand pages!'

'Eleven-hundred and fifty-five, to be precise,' Challenger boomed, 'but I kept it purposely . . . slim. Only the essential information. Now read! Read it all! I will not comment one iota upon my discovery until you have read it all!'

Watson gulped, opened the binder, and flipped through the pages. They were for the most part covered with the most obtuse and complicated mathematical calculations. Even Watson, an educated and scientific medical man, could barely make head or tail of them. He looked imploringly at Holmes for some aid.

Sherlock Holmes simply smiled, opened his book, and began reading. Watson shook his head, giving up on any assistance from his friend, and tried to get through the first-page introductory preface. He soon found himself totally at sea. Astronomy and solar calculations were not his strong point; he only wondered why Holmes was going through with this charade.

'Delve into it, Watson,' Holmes boasted in good humour. 'It makes for fascinating reading. The professor has come up with a theory that I feel will rock the very foundations of our conventional knowledge about the *Titanic* disaster.'

'Really, Holmes?' Watson asked somewhat dubiously.

'Absolutely, my good man. It is all there plainly written in black and white.'

'That it is, Mr. Holmes,' Challenger allowed, now in a far better humour that his work was being accepted and even praised. 'I am gratified to find you appreciating my discovery.'

'I am enjoying it immensely,' Holmes stated in all seriousness as he turned the page and began reading anew. Watson noted his friend was already a few pages ahead of him into his tome, while he was still struggling through page one of his own mammoth volume.

Challenger sat facing the two men in his chair like a statue, unmoving, his eyes firmly fixed upon his guests before him. Every once and a while Holmes would look up, look over at the professor, then look round the house and yard as if digesting the data. Watson merely rubbed his eyes and yearned for the straight-ahead simplicity of the articles in the *Lancet*.

'It does bring thoughtfulness to the mind, does it not, Mr. Holmes?' Challenger asked with obvious delight.

'Indeed it does, Professor. Like all great writing, it must be taken in small doses and digested properly, so its full impact can be properly appreciated.'

Challenger beamed. Someone actually understood his work! He sat back in his chair, with a broad smile breaking through the darkness of his great black beard.

Of course Holmes had noticed the man lurking in the bushes. He had been watching him, and the knife he held intently, for the last few minutes — but he waited.

Suddenly the intruder sprang from the bushes and ran towards the professor. The man — certainly the assassin — held a knife, but Sherlock Holmes had his own weapon. The great detective allowed one immeasurable second to pass as the assassin drew closer to his target — then he acted. It all happened so fast that Watson barely noticed a thing; and Challenger, whose back was towards the assassin, had absolutely no warning at all.

Once the intruder was within range and behind the professor, ready to plunge his knife into the great man's back, Holmes immediately flung the heavy book he had been reading in a mighty upward arc, and it came down precisely upon the assassin's head with a resounding blow. It was like being hit with a cinder block, and the assassin went down to the ground unconscious and bloody.

'Holmes!' Watson shouted in shock.

'My God! What's happened?' Challenger growled. 'Not another annoying newshound?'

'Not a newshound this time, Professor, but your assassin,' Holmes stated as he went over to examine the unconscious man. The weighty book had hit the intruder squarely in the head; he would be out for some time. 'Watson, please be so kind as to ask the professor's wife to phone the police.'

'Of course, Holmes,' Watson said, then set off on his errand.

'Holmes?' Challenger asked, noticing the knife on the ground near the man's hand, which the great detective now picked up and examined. 'I admit I did not believe you. Now I must. How did you spot him?'

'This lovely patio garden makes a perfect location for a murder. All these bushes that surround the house offer any attacker plenty of camouflage. Of course, I noticed the fellow lurking there immediately we came out here, but I knew you would require proof there was serious danger. That is why I was so agreeable to Watson and I reading your books. That gave me time to keep track of the man, and for him to launch his attack.

In the end, if nothing else, your book made a most effective weapon.'

'Aye, it just proves that my research does have its uses, eh, Mr. Holmes?' Challenger's voice enthused with joy rather than insult at the remark. 'But who is he, and why the attack upon my person?'

'If I am not very much mistaken, he is a Serbian national, but we may find there are German masters behind him. You are working on some problems for the Admiralty on a new underwater vessel, a submersible, are you not?'

'Why yes, but that is top secret,' Challenger stated guardedly.

'My brother informed me about it. The German navy is likewise working upon such a vessel, what they call a U-boat.'

'Ah yes, the *unterseeboot*. So they seek to put a stop to my work?'

'Precisely,' Holmes stated as he bound the still-unconscious assassin so that he presented a neat package ready for the police. 'Now perhaps you will allow the police protection that Malone and my brother have insisted upon?'

'Aye, Mr. Holmes, I will most certainly allow it now.'

Watson and Jessie Challenger ran out of the house, Jessie to embrace her husband in tears of joy and relief, the doctor to Holmes.

'I called Lestrade, and he will be here soon to take the assassin away,' Watson said. 'I am sure the man will have much explaining to do.'

5. The Professor's Finding

It was now late afternoon, and all the excitement of the morning was over. The assassin had been taken away by Scotland Yard, and the Challenger home at Enmore Park was once again back to normal.

'You still have not finished reading my findings, Mr. Holmes, Doctor Watson,' Challenger said in a most insistent tone. 'Before you leave for London, you should experience all that my research has established.'

Watson gave an audible moan and

looked pleadingly at his friend, whispering, 'Please, Holmes, don't let him make me read that entire thing.'

Sherlock Holmes smiled at the doctor and looked meaningfully at Professor Challenger. 'I suggest a synopsis of your findings might be best, straight from your own lips. That would be far more effective, and put this entire matter into perspective far better than any mere text ever could.'

'You do not want to read the entire book?' Challenger asked, somewhat chastened.

'Well, actually no, Professor. In any event, poor Watson here would not understand it; and speaking for myself, my own abilities in astronomy and among the higher mathematics is severely limited. I am, after all, no Professor Moriarty.'

'Hah! That fraud!' Challenger boomed in anger.

'Nevertheless a brilliant man, and his treatise upon the binomial theorem — '

'Which he stole from me!' Challenger barked, now flaring rage. 'Just as he stole my notes for his much vaulted book, *The Dynamics of an Asteroid*!'

'Most interesting. I had no idea. Well, in any event, he is long gone now,' Holmes added soothingly.

'And good riddance!'

'So what will it be, Professor? A brief explanation? Watson and I would be most grateful to hear it.'

Challenger nodded. 'So be it. Well, where to begin? The *Titanic* tragedy, the sinking of that magnificent ship after hitting an iceberg, the tremendous loss of life . . . Underlying reasons, sir — that is what I was seeking to discover since first I heard news of the great disaster. The more I thought about the tragedy, the more I could not believe such a thing possible. I tell you, it galled me massively. Surely nothing so devastating had ever happened before in maritime history. So, then, there had to be some reason behind it, and that reason must be exceptional. Then I came upon something extraordinary.'

Challenger stopped his narration, looking off into the sky as if he could see and hear the disaster taking place before him.

'Please continue, Professor,' Holmes prompted.

'What I found,' Challenger stated, as if giving a lecture to two of his students, 'was that climatic conditions were overall responsible for what had occurred. Specifically, exceptionally strong tides allowed the iceberg field to form which struck the *Titanic*. Now, icebergs have been known to be a menace in those north Atlantic waters for decades by seamen. The captain of the ship even set his course in a more southerly direction to avoid them. However, my research shows a convergence of three astronomical events which exaggerated the effects of tidal forces upon the Atlantic Ocean.'

Challenger took a deep breath, then continued, 'It was a unique combination of these three astronomical events. You see, the moon was full on January the fourth, which created what we call a spring tide. That means the tide-raising forces combine to greater net effect. At the same time, the moon was at perigee — at its closest point to the earth. This caused an eccentric orbit that enhanced the gravitational pull on our planet. The earth was also at perihelion — its closest point to the sun. This boosts the sun's gravitational influence.'

'I fail to see ... ' Watson said impatiently.

'Bear with me, Doctor,' Challenger demanded in a surprisingly patient tone. 'It was all due to the increased tidal force created on January the fourth and the perigees of December sixth and February second — these effects raised the sea level, which refloated hundreds of icebergs that had been held fast in the low waters off the Greenland coast. Some of them held for many years, in fact. Because of these events, and the higher than normal tides, these icebergs broke free to float south, eventually to doom the unlucky ship. The *Titanic* blindly cruised under the pitch-blackness of a dark moon that fateful night straight into a field of hundreds, if not thousands, of deadly iceberg traps. I am afraid there could have been no other result.'

'Amazing, Professor!' Watson cried.

Then he added sadly, 'So the poor ship had no chance?'

Sherlock Holmes nodded gravely. 'No chance at all. It is a powerful theory, Professor.'

'Aye, powerful, Mr. Holmes; but no one will believe it, I am afraid. Leastways not today, or tomorrow, but perhaps someday they will.'

'Someday,' Holmes stated, 'we will possess the science to prove your calculations. Then history shall record that it was the power of the moon and tides that set into motion events that sank the ship that was called unsinkable — R.M.S. *Titanic*. You have done exceptional work, sir.'

Challenger beamed. 'As have you, and Doctor Watson. I thank you both most gratefully. You stopped an assassination attempt that surely, if successful, would have severely interfered with my work — and no doubt caused my dearest Jessie undue distress.'

'I am sure such an event would upset her most severely,' Holmes added with a slim smile, then added, 'Professor, it has been a pleasure to make your acquaintance and to learn the truth behind the *Titanic* tragedy.'

'Not bad for an honest day's work, eh, Mr. Holmes? Just wait until Malone hears of this!'

HISTORICAL NOTE:
Much research has been done into the sinking of R.M.S. *Titanic*. Books abound, and theories do as well. Many are interesting but inconclusive. Challenger's findings, presented by him in this story set in 1913, had to wait almost a hundred years before being verified by science. In 1995, Fergus Wood suggested the moon's perigee of January 4, 1912 may have had a role in the sinking of the great ship by freeing up the icebergs from the Jakobshaun Glacier in Greenland. Further research was more recently done by Don Olson, Russell Doescher and Roger Sinnott for their article in *Sky & Telescope* magazine's April 2012 issue entitled 'Did The Moon Sink The Titanic?'. It offers a fascinating and very plausible theory on just what might have

happened to allow the deadly iceberg to meet the ill-fated luxury liner. The rest, as they say, is history.

THE CELLAR AT NO.5

Shelley Smith

Mrs. Rampage lives alone, in a large house cluttered with her precious objets d'art. Her daughter is half a world away, and her niece has no time for the old lady. So Mrs. Rampage is persuaded — much against her will — to take a companion into her home: Mrs. Roach, a poor but respectable widow. As resentment mounts between the pair, a violent confrontation is inevitable when the suppressed tension finally boils over . . .

SHERLOCK HOLMES AND MR. MAC

Gary Lovisi

'Mr. Mac', as Sherlock Holmes calls him, is the talented young Inspector Alec MacDonald. Though he's out to make his mark at Scotland Yard, some baffling new cases have him seeking assistance from the great detective; and the two, along with the stalwart Doctor Watson, join forces. In *The Affair of Lady Westcott's Lost Ruby*, the seemingly mundane disappearance of an elderly lady's pet leads to unexpectedly sinister consequences, while in *The Unseen Assassin*, a mysterious marksman embarks upon a serial killing spree across London.